"Suppose I promise to make you happy?"

"You couldn't," she said quickly. "I hate you. I hate you because you've forced your way into my life, because you've taken everything from me. How can you make anyone happy? You're not even real. You're just raw power."

His eyes ran over her darkly and she shivered as his hand slowly rose to touch her skin. His fingertips rested lightly on the frantic pulse at the base of her throat as if he were listening to her innermost thoughts.

"Then I'll not promise anything," James assured her quietly. "I'll simply wait. You'll come to me, Gemma, because you need me."

PATRICIA WILSON used to live in Yorkshire, England, but with her children all grown up, she decided to give up her teaching position there and accompany her husband on an extended trip to Spain. Their travels are providing her with plenty of inspiration for her romance writing.

Books by Patricia Wilson

HARLEQUIN PRESENTS
1430—STORMY SURRENDER
1454—CURTAIN OF STARS
1469—THE GIFT OF LOVING
1518—PERILOUS REFUGE
1547—FORBIDDEN ENCHANTMENT
1564—JUNGLE ENCHANTMENT

HARLEQUIN ROMANCE
2856—BRIDE OF DIAZ
3102—BOND OF DESTINY

Don't miss any of our special offers. Write to us at the following address for information on our newest releases.

Harlequin Reader Service
P.O. Box 1397, Buffalo, NY 14240
Canadian address: P.O. Box 603,
Fort Erie, Ont. L2A 5X3

PATRICIA WILSON

Intangible Dream

Harlequin Books

TORONTO • NEW YORK • LONDON
AMSTERDAM • PARIS • SYDNEY • HAMBURG
STOCKHOLM • ATHENS • TOKYO • MILAN
MADRID • WARSAW • BUDAPEST • AUCKLAND

Harlequin Presents first edition August 1993
ISBN 0-373-11578-4

Original hardcover edition published in 1992
by Mills & Boon Limited

INTANGIBLE DREAM

CHAPTER ONE

IT WAS raining at the funeral—no great downpour, but the steady, even drizzle of grey skies weeping over the grave. Somebody came and held an umbrella over Gemma but she hardly noticed. Her eyes were dry, her tears had already been shed and she stared down, her mind anaesthetised against further hurt by the cold, numb horror of grief. She could hear the vicar's voice droning on, set words that meant nothing to her. Her father was dead, his last days touched by scandal.

How many people here were thinking about it? How many so-called friends and business acquaintances were standing here and longing to see tomorrow's papers? She threw back her head and looked round, preparing to meet their eyes, her pale face composed.

Grief was private, tears were shed in secret and she had done her weeping already. They looked away. A few held her gaze for a second but even the toughest had to drop their eyes before the blaze of pride on that beautiful face. All except one.

James Sanderson stood away from the rest of the mourners but, even so, he seemed to tower over them, his height topping the other men present by inches. His dark eyes held hers with no apology, no embarrassment. Dominating, arrogant and unsmiling, it was a face she had come to fear.

He was almost lethally powerful, tall, broad-shouldered, an immaculate, perfect physique, dark hair and eyes that now looked like black ice as they watched her. Was he waiting for her to break, to collapse? She knew those eyes; they were extraordinary, deep brown, the sort of eyes you could sink into and never get out of. They gave nothing away. His expression never gave anything away either. He was hard and perfect as polished marble.

The vicar stepped in front of her, breaking the dark spell, and she listened patiently to his inadequate words. Who could comfort her? There was no one, not now. Her life seemed to have ended days ago, ended when her father died. Now there was the house—Brightways—beautiful and empty, no longer hers. When it had gone there would be nothing left at all.

'Miss Lyle. I didn't really know your father...' The vicar watched her a little anxiously, a kindly man who saw the blank despair in her eyes.

'*I* knew him.' Her voice was flat, utterly lifeless, and he tried again because he had to.

'If you need help, advice...'

'She has help. It's kind of you, of course, but I will deal with Miss Lyle's affairs. There really is no need to worry.'

Gemma looked up at the sound of the deep, dark voice, a voice that perfectly matched the man, and James Sanderson stood by her, overwhelming her, intimidating, something almost primitive in the intensity of his command. For a moment a feeling of utter vulnerability flickered through her as if he had authority over each breath she took. Words of denial rose in her throat but they were never spoken.

'I'll take you home, Gemma.' His hand closed over her arm and he turned her away, his mastery swirling around her.

'I—I can't...' Her eyes turned back to the grave, disbelief and pain suddenly animating her face, but he urged her on relentlessly.

'He's gone, Gemma. You have to go home. Time will ease things.'

'How would you know? You're like granite—unfeeling, hard. Who have you ever loved?'

Because they were the focus of many eyes she kept her voice low, but there was a mounting bitterness that he heard only too well.

'Rage at me if you want to. I can take it. Just keep that face composed, though, and your voice down until we're clear of here. The Press hounds are out and at least two photographers are in the trees.' His voice was cold, warning, and his grip tightened like steel. He didn't have to repeat himself. She knew. She had already seen them and she was Gemma Lyle, fair game for the Press. She took a deep, steadying breath, her fair head lifting again, her face quite still and controlled.

'Good girl,' he murmured quietly. 'Just keep it up until we're out of here.'

He ignored the car that had brought her, dismissing the chauffeur with one wave of his hand. There was a stream of cars, black, funereal, filling the lane to the small church, but somehow he had managed to get his great silver Mercedes in by the gate, although it had not been there before. Tiredly, she wondered about it. Had he ordered someone away? It wasn't at all unlikely. He was James Sanderson, sure of his world, dominant, handsome, virile and cold as black stone.

He helped her into the warmth and luxury of the car and then pulled away, gathering speed rapidly, his eyes flicking to the rear-view mirror, and Gemma too saw the flurry of activity as the waiting Press took last-minute shots, cursing themselves, no doubt, that they had not tried to interview her during the funeral.

'They'll be up at the house soon enough,' she sighed, resting her head back wearily on the deep leather of the seat.

'Not with the gates locked,' he said coldly.

'How can I lock the gates? People will be coming up to the house, expecting a drink, commiserating...'

'Prying,' he finished sardonically. 'They won't. I cancelled all that.'

'You did *what*?' She sat up straight and stared at him, but his eyes merely flared over her icily.

'I've spoken to people. Those who were your father's friends understand only too well how you feel and they know the ability of the Press to squeeze in where water can't seep. They approve. The others are unimportant. Nobody is going into Brightways except you and me. As for the gates, I brought two of the men down with me. The Press will stay out.'

She saw what he meant as the car swung into the driveway of Brightways. The men were big, tough, construction workers from the firm, and no words were wasted. He nodded at them and they nodded back. She heard the gates swing shut and the dull clang was as final as her life seemed to be.

'A few more enemies made,' she pointed out drily, and he glanced across at her with dark, still eyes.

'Enemies don't bother me. I grew up in a tough world, Miss Lyle. Right now, be thankful of it. Good breeding is not really a lot of help in the jungle.'

'You mean I'm spoiled, puerile, soft all the way through?'

'A social success and a lightweight as far as the real world is concerned,' he agreed derisively. 'You have two things going for you. You're beautiful and your father loved you. He was my friend. I'll protect you all I can.'

'I don't need——' she began hotly, but as usual he never even let her finish.

'You don't need the help of a tough nobody who clawed his way from the gutter?' he enquired sarcastically. 'Don't overstate your case too soon. Learn caution. The party's over.'

There was something in his voice that brought a wave of alarm and Gemma looked across at him quickly, but the dark, handsome face was utterly still, his eyes on the curving length of the drive. The hard, carved lips were uncompromising and she felt the slow closing of the doors of a trap.

He was utterly ruthless, everyone knew that. Her father had held him in great esteem and James Sanderson was no stranger to Brightways. But Gemma had often felt herself almost choking when he was invited, only her love of her father and her duty as his hostess making her able to stay in the same room.

The dark, imperious power frightened her. The dark, intent eyes frightened her. Beneath the polish, the gloss, the sophistication he was a savage and she knew it. He had carved his name in big letters in the business world and she had never doubted her father's assertion that James Sanderson was a brilliant engineer. She knew he could work on after other people dropped. She knew he had almost uncanny business acumen and had built a fortune on it, but to her he was like an untamed jungle cat, the veneer of civilisation only very thin. Cross him and he would destroy you.

Barry Lyle had laughed at her fancies and she could still hear his voice now.

'Darling! James is an educated man. Don't mistake his lowly beginnings for stupidity. He won scholarships from being a boy and he worked damned hard. He had to. There were no private schools for James, no tennis-club parties, not much recreation at all, I would think, although he was a first-class rugby player and could have been a professional from all I hear.'

'I suppose you hear it from him?'

'Don't be scathing, Gemma, love. James never talks about himself. He works too hard to waste time with words. I'm thankful he came into the firm. He didn't need to.'

No, he hadn't needed to. James Sanderson had a civil-engineering firm that seemed to span the world. He had started from nothing and he was already wealthy when he turned his eye on Lyle Engineering. Now it was Sanderson-Lyle, part of his group but left with a slightly different name. Her father had said it sounded better that way but Gemma knew that James Sanderson had poured money into the firm and had soon had control. He hadn't quite gobbled her father's firm up, merely annexed it, and nobody had been left in doubt as to who was the boss.

She had always resented it. The firm had been in her father's family for generations, comfortable, respected. Gemma had never known any other sort of life but wealth and ease. There had been no outside influence at all until James Sanderson had appeared like a dark, forbidding shadow, his cold, handsome face a shocking reminder that there were wolves 'out there'.

Gemma had never worked; her father would never allow it and she knew James Sanderson despised her—she had always known that. She had also known very soon who really swung the weight in the firm. One glance from him made strong men search their minds for excuses. He alarmed her. He was alarming her now but she was also impatiently grateful for his protection right at this moment.

Tomorrow perhaps she would be able to face things. Her father had lost everything but his share in the firm. Just before he died he had told her. He had lived another life she knew nothing of at all—a yacht, gambling, women. There was nothing left. Even his share in the firm would not cancel out the debts; even selling

Brightways would not really even things up. She had nothing left but her pride and her bitterness because James Sanderson must have known what was going on. He had simply let it happen, waited like a predator, and now he dared to call her father his friend.

The car swung smoothly along and pulled up in front of the house, and Gemma got out to stand for a minute in the slowly falling rain, looking at it as if she would never see it again because soon that would be all too true.

Brightways had always been the very pattern of her life. It stood on the crest of a hill, the view spectacular, the house also bordering on the spectacular. It was huge and imposing, the walls covered with Virginia creeper, giving it a mellow look that softened the grandeur. She didn't remember any other home at all. To leave here would be the final blow and at the moment she felt it would crush her.

She had forgotten that James Sanderson was beside her until he spoke.

'You love this house, don't you?'

'Yes. I've never lived anywhere else. Now I'll have to leave it.'

'That's up to you,' he said coolly, taking her arm and leading her up the steps to the front door.

'I wish it were.' She gave a strange little laugh. 'I think I'd keep it if I had to live in one room and eat only twice a week. Everything in my life that was good happened in this house. When Brightways goes, every last thing goes too, including the memories.'

'Memories are in the mind.'

'Is that why you're so cold?' She suddenly wanted to hurt him because she was hurt, and that was funny—as if anyone could hurt him! 'No, that was idiotic—forget it. Nothing could hurt you. You're invincible, aren't you?'

'Is that how you think of me? Invincible?' He had one of those strange smiles on his lips that always worried her—secret, dark, as if he was thinking things she couldn't possibly imagine.

'I don't *ever* think of you, Mr Sanderson.'

'That must comfort you, surely? Let's get in out of the rain.' His low growl chilled her even more and his suggestion was backed up by a steely grip that led her onwards.

Jessie appeared as they came into the hall, her face almost as grey as her straight hair. She had always been with them, since Gemma was a little girl, and now she too would have to leave this house. She had been crying, that was easy enough to see, and Gemma went to her impulsively, putting her arms round the drooping shoulders.

'Just you and I, Jessie,' she said quietly, tears in her own eyes.

'Aye, love. We'd better face it. We'll have to find another place to live too.' There were no secrets from Jessie. Her position was more than that of any mere housekeeper. She had almost brought Gemma up.

'I'll have to look for a flat, somewhere we can both squeeze into,' Gemma muttered desperately. 'Your wages, though...'

'You can forget about that! I'll get a job too. We'll pull through.'

'Oh, Jessie! As if I'd let you.' Tears escaped from Gemma's eyes and trickled down her cheeks, and James Sanderson intervened impatiently.

'Make us some tea, Jess. We'll be in the study.'

He was unsmiling, almost curt, but he got the usual smile from Jessie. She liked him and had never been able to fathom Gemma's total aversion to the tall, handsome man. He was the only one who ever called her Jess, and she took it as a compliment. She could see

the steel in him. She too had started life in poverty and
she admired him immensely.

'It's not *the* study,' Gemma pointed out sharply as
Jessie moved away in instant obedience. 'It's my father's
study, and right now I don't want to go in there.'

'If it were not necessary I wouldn't suggest it. We have
things to discuss that need privacy.'

'Privacy! From Jessie? There's nobody else in the
house and she knows everything.'

'There are some things you may not want her to know.'
For a moment he stared down at her, his dark eyes utterly
unfathomable. 'Dry your eyes,' he said abruptly, and
simply walked off to the study, leaving her to follow or
not as she wished.

It infuriated her. Now there was no need whatever for
him to be here. She was grateful for the rescue but now
he should go. He had no idea how she was hurting
because such things would never occur to him. With her
father gone, James Sanderson was no longer welcome
in this house. Until things were settled and it was sold,
this was *her* house and, as far as she was concerned, he
had never been welcome. He had nothing to do with her
at all.

She followed him to tell him that but something about
him stilled her tongue. He was standing looking out of
the window, his eyes on the garden and the fading light,
and she found her glance running over him anxiously.
He was such a power, so much driving energy that she
rarely thought of the man himself. From first meeting
him she had shivered when he looked at her, avoiding
the deep brown eyes as often as possible, but now she
saw his dark, frightening splendour, a superb, masculine
grace.

Plenty of women tried to catch James Sanderson's eye
and Gemma had always privately thought they must be
mad. Now for a second she saw him as they did. She

wondered how he behaved with people he liked. He had
liked her father, called him his friend, and they had
laughed together. She hadn't liked that because it seemed
to bring him closer to her own world, and he was danger.

He suddenly swung round and looked at her, dark
eyes raking over her, taking in the pale oval of her face,
the shoulder-length honey-blonde hair now tied severely
on top of her head. Her eyes were very rare, purple with
small flecks of gold, and at the moment they seemed to
be filling her face.

'You should eat,' he said curtly, his dark brows
gathering in a frown.

'I couldn't.'

'For how long? If you lose any more weight you'll
disappear.' His eyes flared over her slender figure.
'You've reached the point of fragility.'

Gemma sank to a chair, her fingers at her temples,
her eyes closed.

'I need an aspirin more than food.' She was just about
to confess to a headache of major proportions when he
walked out of the room, and it brought on a small rueful
smile. Imagine telling James Sanderson you had a
headache! It was like telling some great deity about a
slightly sore toe. Jessie brought the tea but James was
right behind her and she didn't linger.

'Take these.' He startled Gemma by putting two tablets
into her hand and she just stared up at him, her eyes
narrowed with pain.

'What are they?'

'Perfectly safe,' he rasped. 'Not something I had
manufactured to dispose of you. Jessie got them out of
her own cabinet when I mentioned your headache.' He
poured the tea and handed her a cup. 'Take them now.'

She murmured her thanks and swallowed them, feeling
guilty and ungrateful, but then, part of his danger was
that you never knew what he would do next. He leaned

forward and pulled the band from her hair, frowning as the honey-blonde mass of it swung around her face.

'Having your hair screwed up on top isn't helping any,' he muttered. 'Leave it be!' he added harshly as she nervously smoothed it back. 'Get your drink and then we'll talk.'

'About what? I know the lot. Daddy explained it all before he died. There's nothing more you can tell me because I can't lose more than everything and I've lost that.'

'Well, you're not a little rich girl any more,' he agreed irascibly, angered, no doubt, by her tone.

'And you think I care?' Her voice rose sharply and she jumped up. 'He's gone! Gone! Nothing and nobody can replace him.'

She turned away, hiding her face, her shoulders bent as she gave way again to deep, black grief and she hardly noticed when he came to her swiftly and gathered her into hard, strong arms. She never thought about who it was, the utter incongruity of it; all she needed was comfort, and comfort was there, strength and power an iron wall around her.

For a few blind minutes she sobbed heartbrokenly and he simply let her, holding her fast, and then she tried to move, shame and a flicker of utter disbelief bringing her back to the present.

'I—I'm sorry...'

'Don't be. It's part of healing.' He looked down at her, his arms still loosely around her. She felt like a butterfly pinned to a card. He had never touched her before, except to shake her hand that first time her father had invited him home, and now she was aware of his strength and her own fragility. She was quite powerless to move unless he released her, odd feelings flicking along her veins. 'How old are you, Gemma?'

'Twenty-four.'

His lips twisted wryly. 'Twenty-four. To look as you do in the world I came from you would have had to be about fifteen. My mother died when she was thirty-nine. She looked like an old woman.'

He turned away, letting her go, and she watched him with wide, tear-wet eyes.

'How old were you then?'

'Nineteen. I was at university. I never went back home again. Luckily I was an only child so there were no responsibilities for me.'

'Your father...?'

'Was a confirmed drunk and bully, well practised.'

'I—I'm sorry.'

'Are you?' He turned and looked at her, his face hard, just as it always seemed to be when he looked at her. It was unbelievable that he had just told her about his past, more unbelievable still that he had comforted her, but she could see it didn't signify any chink in his armour. 'Don't waste pity on me, Gemma. It's a long time since I was poor. I've even forgotten. Maybe your tears reminded me. Normally I don't have much patience with tears.'

'You didn't have to be here to watch mine,' she began defensively.

'They were for a man I liked. Very forgivable. Anyway, your father was my partner. I owe you some responsibility.' He sat down and motioned her sternly to her seat. 'Sit and finish your tea. Then we'll talk.'

'What could we possibly have to talk about?' She sat down and smoothed her hair back in the same nervous manner, everything inside her strung to breaking-point.

'We've managed well enough so far,' he pointed out ironically. 'More words than you've said to me in the two years I've known you.'

'So? The words are said now.' She looked down to escape the dark eyes. 'There's nothing else to discuss.'

'Oh, yes, there is,' he assured her firmly. 'We're here to discuss you.'

'Me?' She looked up quickly, the purple of her eyes deepening. 'I'm nothing to you, no responsibility at all. I'm not a child who needs looking after and, in any case, my father was only your partner in Sanderson-Lyle—a mere pen-stroke on your great portfolio.'

Her voice was edged with bitterness and she knew it. Even now, when the firm was no longer anything to do with her, she resented the fact that the name was changed, that Sanderson was added, dominating it just as James Sanderson dominated everything he touched.

If he heard the bitterness he chose to ignore it. He leaned back and stretched out long, strong legs, looking completely at ease while she sat on the edge of her seat, quivering with tension. He watched her for a minute, his eyes running over her quite comprehensively until she was almost rigid with anxiety. The hard, sensuous lips suddenly twisted in amusement at the way she was looking at him, spellbound by his authority in spite of her deeply rooted antagonism.

'What are your plans?' he asked coolly and, although she knew she should be telling him to mind his own business, she couldn't. He was her father's partner, anyhow. When the Lyle half of the firm was sold off, James Sanderson would have a lot of wheeling and dealing to do to get another partner he could work with even if he did own most of the firm already.

'I'll stay here until the house is sold, as long as they'll let me, anyhow. Meanwhile I'll look for a flat big enough for Jessie and me. It will have to be in London because I won't be able to afford many train fares for a while.' She spread her hands with delicate helplessness. 'I don't know how long it will be before they start sorting things out...I mean...'

'You mean you've never been mixed up in anything sordid before in your life.'

Her head shot up at the cold derision. 'Did you expect me to have experience of things like this—me, a lightweight?' Her face was flushed and angry but he merely looked at her steadily, not rising to any bait.

'Actually, you're mixed up in nothing at all. The eager actions of the Press are all a waste of effort, merely because my name is linked with the firm. Had it been just your father I'm sure his death would have gone unnoticed by the tabloids. As it is, there may be a couple of days of colourful speculation. Barry's secret lifestyle may be brought out into the open, and possibly some of the women he knew will be willing to sell their stories. If they're looking for any business scandal, however, facts will soon stop that. Your father's debts are settled. Nothing further is about to happen.'

'What do you mean?' He wasn't a man to make foolish jokes, but she couldn't absorb what he was telling her, and he shrugged dismissively.

'Weeks before he died, your father wanted to see me. He also wanted Denby, your solicitor. We worked out a deal. On the day he died we came again and it was all finalised.'

'What do you mean—a deal?' She was frightened again, on the edge of something she couldn't quite grasp.

'I bought out your father's share of the firm. Cheques have already gone out. There are no debts.'

'But even that wouldn't be enough...'

'I also bought the house. Brightways is mine.'

'So you did it? You finally got everything! A cold rush of anger raced over her and Gemma sprang up, her face white as a sheet. 'The moment I saw you I knew you were dangerous, but he wouldn't even listen to me. You must have known how things were going, but you just sat back and let it happen, waiting for the right moment to plunder. Now you've got everything—and he's dead.'

She never even thought deeply about what she was saying until she saw the harsh fury on his face, until he slowly rose to his full, forbidding height and looked down at her with icy eyes.

'Be very careful how you speak to me, Miss Lyle. I don't pander to hysterics. What exactly did I do? Did I buy a yacht called *Dream World*? Did I introduce him to almost every casino around the Mediterranean? Did I produce the women?'

Gemma winced and turned away, her face twisted in enough pain to drown her rage, but James grasped her shoulders, spinning her to face him.

'Yes! That's the deepest cut, isn't it? The women!'

'My mother was beautiful...'

'Like you,' he rasped. 'I know that. Barry had a photograph of her in every place he went—his desk at work, here...' He strode round to the desk and pulled open the top drawer violently, taking out a framed photograph and thrusting it into her hands. 'Madeleine!' he bit out. 'I know her. I see her every time I look at you. She died a very long time ago, but not to him. My God! To love a woman as much as that must be a life sentence.'

'Then why the women?' Gemma took a struggling breath that hurt, and looked at the photograph, the gently smiling face, that fair, shining hair, and James turned away impatiently.

'An anaesthetic, I would think. Certainly they meant nothing to him. There was only Madeleine and you. Every time he saw you he must have seen her—a comfort and a torture. I imagine that from time to time things just snapped.'

He turned back to her irritably.

'This is getting us nowhere. Barry had no idea he was so ill until almost too late, and then he was only

concerned for you—panic-stricken, in fact. That's what
the deal was about and I agreed to three conditions. One,
the firm is to keep its name—Sanderson-Lyle. Two, you
are to have access to Brightways for as long as you wish.'

'As if I'd want that!' Gemma cried hotly. From wealth
and ease she was now poor, not really knowing what to
do at all. Shame at his knowledge of her vulnerability
made her face flush, heightened her anger. 'It's yours
now. You own everything. I'll leave tomorrow.'

He shrugged coldly, utterly impervious to anything she
said. 'I told you as we came in, it's up to you.'

'So what is the last condition? I might as well know
that.' She tossed her head proudly, facing him when she
wanted to run.

'The last condition depends on you. He wanted a
future for you, a good future. I agreed to marry you.'

It was said coldly and flatly, with such obvious lack
of interest that for a moment she felt she had not heard
properly. She just stared at him blankly, not really
thinking at all about the implications, and then every
last bit of colour left her face.

'Y-you . . . agreed . . . t-to . . . ?'

'It suits me well enough,' he informed her indiffer-
ently, his face quite expressionless. 'It gave him peace
at the end and I have no great objections.'

Horror, incredulity and panic washed over Gemma and
showed all too readily on her face. She took a small step
away from him and then gave a soft moan and slid to
the deeply carpeted floor in a faint.

When she came round she was lying on the settee and
James was sitting beside her, watching her with dark eyes
that seemed to probe her soul.

'Neat,' he congratulated sarcastically. 'No fuss, no
screams, just instant oblivion. I'll try it at the next
awkward board meeting. Not that you really astonished

me,' he added severely. 'You look as if you've been eating what the sparrows left over.'

He got up and poured her a small brandy, coming back to hold it out to her, but she seemed incapable of even taking it from his hand.

'Where's your courage?' he taunted cruelly. 'If you accidentally touch my hand you'll not be compromised in any way at all.' It shamed her into taking the glass, but it shook so much in her hand that James reached out with a look of impatience and held it, lifting her until she could drink.

'Y-you don't have to...'

'I don't have to do anything,' he agreed irascibly, 'although I suppose, theoretically, I could toss you out into the night and wheedle Jessie to stay.'

'Please be serious.' She touched his hand quite without thought and he looked down imperiously at the pale fingers against his tanned skin, making her snatch her hand away speedily. 'I'd like to get up.'

'Very well. But I'm warning you to stay right there on the settee for a while. You look very shaken.'

'Are you surprised?' She swung her legs to the floor but remained where she was, and he gave a hard laugh.

'No, I'm not surprised. There wasn't any other way of telling you. Creeping up on you with the idea was clearly a waste of time. I'm not in any doubt about what you think of me, Gemma. You've gone to a lot of trouble to make it quite plain over the past two years and I'm not exactly what you're used to.'

'Then why did you even bother to mention it?'

'Because I gave my word and, as I informed you before your dramatic slide into unconsciousness, it suits me well enough.'

'How can it suit you? I don't like you at all. Is it likely that I'd agree?'

'Look!' He spun round on her so suddenly that she jumped, and that didn't please him either; his dark eyes burned her. 'I'm thirty-five, successful, wealthy and un-married. I intend to live at Brightways. This house has always appealed to me, and naturally, I need a hostess. I've seen you in action here; nobody could do it better.'

'I—I don't think you really know what you're saying,' Gemma began desperately. 'People don't get married for that sort of reason.'

'No,' he agreed coldly. 'They get married for the reason your father married his Madeleine. Endless love, except that it never is, for a variety of reasons. I had a tough beginning, Miss Lyle. I have no intention of having a tough end. This is a business deal, part of the bargain I made with your father. No love, no grief. I want a beautiful wife who appreciates beautiful things, who is accustomed to wealth and values it. You will have every-thing you want. You will have luxury and safety. You will have my name but you will not have me.'

'I don't want you!' Gemma snapped. 'I disliked you on sight.'

'Why?'

His sudden, quiet question baffled her, and she blushed softly. 'How can you explain something like that? It was instinctive. I recognised you—somehow. I saw you for what you are.'

'And what am I, Gemma? I already know I'm a tough nobody.'

'I never said that. In fact I never even thought it.'

'Then why the dislike?'

'You're danger. I knew it as soon as I saw you. I can see it now.' She found herself looking into his eyes. He had come back to sit beside her and those dark eyes were drowning her. His mouth tilted in amusement and to her embarrassment he trailed one long finger down her cheek.

'You *are* unworldly, Miss Lyle. You have a wild imagination.'

'I have a great sense of self-preservation.' She snatched her face away, blushing again, blushing even more when he laughed softly. 'I don't really want to talk about this, if you don't mind. And in any case,' she added, a thought suddenly striking her, 'what about Miss Prescott, your...?'

'Mistress?' he enquired helpfully. 'Don't be afraid to speak right out. Harsh words can't damage Roma.'

CHAPTER TWO

GEMMA hadn't imagined they could. The papers had spent a good deal of time lately following James's progress with Roma Prescott, owner of a chain of successful boutiques that looked as if they were going to span the country. A female entrepreneur, glossy and sharp as a bag of razors, her exploits in the business world had enthralled the Press. She didn't look as if anything could hurt her.

'I'm not interested in damaging her, or in anything else, for that matter. I just want to wake up and find that it's all a terrible dream.'

'No wonder your father was in a panic about you,' James suddenly snapped, getting up to pace away from her. 'You're quite unreal. How do imagine you're going to survive? You've never done a real day's work in your life. You're planning to take a run-down flat in a sleazy neighbourhood and fill it with *nouveau* second-hand furniture?'

'There's furniture here...'

'So there is, but it's mine. You estimated that selling the house wouldn't even settle the debts, and you were right. I bought the furniture too. Antiques are valuable; it just about squared everything up.'

'So I have nothing,' she whispered, and he spun round to glare at her.

'You can have your clothes—if you can find a flat big enough to contain such a large, glamorous wardrobe.'

'You don't know anything about my wardrobe or my lifestyle,' she said resentfully.

One black brow rose derisively. 'I follow your progress. The theatre, the ballet, dinners and dances with upper-crust escorts.' He looked at her sceptically. 'You think you're going to survive with a flat in London? Then what? A job? What sort of a job? All you know is how to look beautiful and how to charm guests and escorts. You might survive a week. It's throwing a lamb to the wolves, a silky little virgin in the big, bad city.'

'You have no idea that I'm . . .' She stopped, blushing hotly, and he suddenly looked wryly amused.

'Indeed I do. You tell me you see danger on my face. I see virginity on yours. And, in any case, I know all about you, Gemma. Your reputation is pure as driven snow.' He stood still and looked down at her with intent eyes. 'You really haven't had much of a life, have you? Barry kept you close and never let you lift a finger to help yourself. He wanted a living image of Madeleine right under his nose. When things got too much for him, he simply went off and blew in a bit more cash, quite secure in the knowledge that you were settled into a safe little life. Even so, he was so far gone with grief that he never thought about your future.'

'You despised him really, didn't you?' Gemma said raggedly, but he shook his dark head and continued to watch her.

'No. I liked him, and I imagine that deep down he knew I'd look out for you when it came down to it. You see, Gemma, it has always been my intention to marry you, right from the moment I first saw you.'

For a minute Gemma just stared at him, her face if anything more pale still. Was this the danger she had instinctively felt? Was this the reason those dark eyes had followed her whenever he was here in this house? Of course not; he was just tightening the noose for reasons of his own. Dignity was the only thing that was going to get her out of this.

'Thank you,' she said quietly. 'I know you're only being kind, although I don't expect it comes easily to you. For some reason you promised my father that you'd marry me and now you're trying to make it sound better. There's really no need to bother. I'll manage quite well. Jessie will be with me and...'

He sat down in the chair opposite and began to laugh, the dark eyes dancing with amusement at her cool, little dignity. She had never seen him laugh like that before and it lit up his face, making him into another person.

'You're quite priceless, Gemma Lyle. Alice in Wonderland, no less.'

'I was only thanking you for your efforts,' Gemma said huffily, and if anything it amused him more.

'And she drew on her gloves and swept out,' he taunted softly. 'Listen, you rare creature. I need a wife and I picked you a long time ago—two years ago, actually. You have everything going for you that I want. You're beautiful, gracious, talented, and you have enough dignity for both of us. This is no new idea. I mentioned it to your father over a year ago.' James grimaced wryly. 'That was a non-starter as far as he was concerned. I was given a brief history of your family background—in a kindly manner, of course. The Lyles are not self-made. The Lyles inherit.' He looked at her quizzically. 'Then, of course, there was Lord William—dear Bill, in your father's words. At the time he was your escort, and I believe Barry might have let you go to a title. At any rate, I didn't merit much thought. He dismissed it from his mind but he remembered at the end when he realised just how vulnerable he was going to leave you. I never dismissed it from my mind because I intended to marry you with or without your father's blessing.'

For a minute Gemma stared at him and he looked back at her with a sort of derisive amusement at the back of his dark eyes. He had never said so much to her

before and had never before even looked as if he wanted
to marry her. What was he up to now?

'You've got to be making this up,' Gemma said hotly.
'Not many minutes ago you told me you wanted a
hostess, and you pointed out your opinion of love!'

'Do you love me?' he asked unexpectedly, his eyes
narrowed in amusement.

'Don't be ridiculous! I don't even like you. I've made
that quite plain.'

'Then let's try to be sensible.' He leaned back and
looked at her levelly, although his lips still twitched in
amusement. 'I've told you why I need a wife and
explained that you're perfect. You need the sort of
background you grew up in, and I can give you that.
You can't survive without me, Gemma.'

'You have a very big opinion of yourself, Mr
Sanderson! Obviously, too, you have a very low opinion
of me. I know you think I'm capable of nothing at all,
but I'm not some Victorian spinster who needs a man
to take care of her.'

She got that slow, dark smile.

'Victorian spinster—a very poor description. I know
you're not capable of fending for yourself. You have
social accomplishments and nothing else. You've been
smothered by kindness all your life. Too much affection
is really enervating and it's probably too late now for
you to stand on your own two feet. Be sensible. You can
live in your own home, live as you've always lived. Jessie
will bless you and, as a matter of fact, so will I.'

'I can't see you stooping to bless anyone,' Gemma
said haughtily. 'You don't need me and I'm not about
to be a sort of poor relation in my own home. I won't
act some dumb hostess with a ring on my finger and one
in my nose, too, by the sound of your proposition.'

'Not a proposition, Gemma. A proposal. I'm a very rich man, even without the firm. I've built a business empire. I need an heir.'

Gemma stood up slowly, almost swaying, and he got to his feet too, the dark eyes observing her intently.

'You said... you said no love. You said you would never feel as my father felt.'

She was terribly frightened suddenly, their conversation until now seeming quite unreal. There was something in his eyes that until this moment had been quite hidden. He wasn't taunting any more and her heart threatened to hammer right out of her body.

'And I never will,' he assured her inexorably. 'Love is not at all necessary. That sort of trap is not for me. I saw my mother trapped and I saw it again with your father.'

'My mother couldn't help dying,' Gemma whispered.

'It sapped his life away and, in some measure, yours too. No woman is going to take my life and then let it drop by leaving me in any way.'

'Then you've got the perfect set-up,' Gemma managed shakily. 'A mistress with the same driving energy, the same selfish desires.'

'So far, it's been enough.' His gaze seemed to concentrate in power until she felt unable to look away. 'Now I want more. I want this house with you in it as I first saw you. I want to own all that cool, golden beauty. I want a child with purple eyes and hair the colour of honey. I want *you*!'

She gave a small, shocked cry and turned to run from the room but he caught her by the waist, spinning her back to him, his arm tightly round her, his other hand spearing into her hair to hold her still.

'I could make you want me,' he threatened darkly. 'I could hold you in my arms until all that virginal terror disappeared, and I wouldn't need love for that. You know nothing of men. Barry saw to that, didn't he? He was scared of losing you. Even at the end he was only happy to hand you over to me because he imagined he knew why I wanted you. He assumed I would keep you safe and unsullied like his china collection, leave you in your old room and simply smile at you across the breakfast table, maybe pat your hand and be quite content to be married to a Lyle. If he'd known what I really wanted he would have simply left things in a mess because nobody had to want his china doll, his little Madeleine.'

'You hated him,' she whispered, her whole body trembling uncontrollably.

'I *knew* him!'

'No. I knew him.' Suddenly she began to cry, hot painful tears that fell on to pale cheeks, choking sobs that welled up from inside. 'Today I buried him.'

He gave a low murmur that might have been either exasperation or pity, she didn't know which, then he swung her up into his arms and walked to the door, her slight weight nothing to his immense strength.

'Jessie!' He shouted just once and instantly Jessie was there, her face anxious and still tear-stained. 'Come and settle her in bed,' he ordered. 'She's had enough.'

He walked up the wide, sweeping staircase, holding Gemma tightly as she tried to get control of her wild weeping, and Jessie ran along in front to open the door of Gemma's room and turn down the sheets. He paused at the door as he walked away again.

'Give her a minute to recover and then feed her,' he commanded. 'She doesn't go to sleep before she's eaten. Much more of this and she's going to be in hospital.'

Seeing him upstairs in this house, hearing him issuing orders just drove home the fact that now he owned everything, controlled everything, and Gemma was silent as Jessie helped her to undress. He was rocking the very foundations of her life. She had to get away and never see him again.

It wasn't that easy. Jessie brought her some soup, a little scrambled egg on toast and a pot of tea, and she was still toying with it when there was a knock on the door and James simply walked in.

'This is my room for now,' she snapped defensively, 'unless, of course, you plan to throw me out tonight?'

'Stop talking nonsense,' he rasped, walking over to look down at her. 'I have no intention whatever of seeing you leave this house and you know it damned well! I came to see if you'd eaten anything. I can see you've moved its position on the plate slightly,' he added, glancing at the tray. 'I'm quite relieved to see that you've finished the soup. Much more of this and I'll have you in hospital anyway.'

'What I do is absolutely none of your concern!' Gemma said tightly, anxiety growing at his attitude. She felt utterly trapped. Everything inside her told her to fight him now or go under, but she was too weary and grieved to fight.

'Everything you do is my concern,' he said sharply. He took the tray and placed it on the small table by the bed and then moved to sit beside her, making her move anxiously further away.

'Will you please go?' He was frightening her even more, making her skin grow hot, and she looked at him wild-eyed, almost pleading.

'For God's sake stop being scared of me!' he growled. 'Do you think I'm planning to rape you and tell Jessie to mind her own business? Believe me, I don't need to use force.'

'I'm sure you don't,' Gemma retaliated, flushing hotly. 'Your love-life has been strewn across the papers for as long as I can remember. I'd have to be illiterate not to know who you've dated these past few years. When Miss

Prescott came on the scene they did a full synopsis of the past.'

'You could easily have turned the page,' he murmured, suddenly sardonically amused. 'You surely didn't feel obliged to read about my indiscretions?'

'I'm not at all interested! Something so blatant, though, is difficult to miss.'

He smiled derisively. 'Never believe all you read in the papers,' he warned softly. 'Plenty of women are prepared to have their name linked with mine on the off-chance it will do them some good. At that point I normally drop them.'

'Everybody knows you're cold-blooded.'

'The ladies don't seem to think so. Or do you imagine it's because of my money?'

'Obviously,' she lied. She knew he had women falling over his feet and she knew it wasn't his money, either. He was dynamic, a frightening sexual attraction hidden behind that imperious face. Until today she had never noticed it because until today she had been just as far away from him as she could get, avoiding his eyes, changing direction when he came towards her at any gathering they had held at Brightways. She had been aloof and distant, keeping him at arm's length.

Tonight, though, he had forced her to look at him. He had forced her to face him and she was more scared than ever, not by his power but by the man himself.

'You're staring at me to look for clues?' he enquired wryly. 'You want me to prove to you that it's not just my money?'

'You're being despicable,' she managed shakily. 'You've got me at a disadvantage and you're showing just what you're really like.'

'You don't know what I'm really like, Gemma,' he assured her softly. His eyes skimmed over her and she was glad that her nightie was not transparent; the white satin covered her well but his eyes found the rather frantic pulse that beat in her throat and he smiled again, that dark, slow smile. 'Virginal,' he murmured. 'I could have expected you to sleep in white.'

'Please go away,' she said in little more than a whisper. 'You have no right to be up here.'

'I've wanted to be up here for a long time.' He held her with dark eyes. 'Frightened little Gemma. Too scared to live. Too protected to learn. Barry did you no favours, really.'

It brought it all tumbling back. Here with him in her room the air seemed to be vibrant but just beyond the door there was silence, there would always be silence.

'I'll never see him again.' She whispered the words and closed her eyes, tears squeezing under her thick, dark lashes.

'He sees you.'

It was so unexpected, so utterly astonishing coming from someone so coldly dynamic, so unfeeling, that she opened her eyes to stare up at him, liquid pools like purple gems flecked with gold. His dark gaze met hers, drowning her, holding her, and she couldn't look away at all.

'Suppose I promise to make you happy?' he asked softly.

'You couldn't. I hate you. I hate you because you've forced your way into my life, because you've taken everything from me. How can you make anyone happy? You're not even real. You're just raw power.'

His eyes ran over her darkly and she shivered as his hand slowly raised to touch her skin. His fingertips rested lightly on the frantic pulse at the base of her throat as if he was listening to her innermost thoughts.

'Then I'll not promise anything,' he assured her quietly. 'I'll simply wait. I've waited two years so far. You'll come to me, Gemma, because you need me.' He stood and looked down at her with the same dark, fathomless eyes she had grown accustomed to. 'In the meantime, I'll make my own arrangements. Tonight, with your permission, I'll sleep at Brightways. The men will stay on the gate until morning, but all the same I have good reason to distrust the Press. Go to sleep. Nothing is going to disturb you.'

He walked out and closed the door and she just sat there staring at it. Everything was going to disturb her. *He* disturbed her. His every word and action was unexpected, his dominance still filled the room. She turned out the lamp and slid down the bed, her mind tormented.

'Oh, Daddy! Daddy! Why?' she whispered brokenly. Whatever he had done, she could never blame him. She was in the power of a dark and dynamic man but she had no thought to blame anyone but James Sanderson. Her slender arm slid from the bed and took the photograph that stood on the cabinet, and she didn't need the light on to see her mother's beautiful face. Was she everything he had said? A china doll? Merely an image of her mother? Tears slid down her cheeks as she fell asleep.

The sound of voices woke Gemma early next day and she got out of bed to look down at the front of the house. There was a car drawn up to the steps and four tough men were talking to James. It only added to the feeling of being under siege—and not only from the Press.

James was dressed and ready for the City and he stood like the wealthy businessman he was, hands in his pockets, the jacket of his dark suit pushed back. She couldn't hear what he was saying but one of those lean brown hands appeared and cut through the air decisively and the men nodded in determined understanding. He was telling them to guard the house and she had the awful feeling that he would be keeping her here too.

She dressed rapidly and went down the stairs. It seemed to be terribly important to be on the spot, to ward off any further plans before they became permanent. For the past two years she had avoided him both at work and here in the house, but now he was unavoidable, impossible to dismiss.

There were voices in the kitchen too, and she veered away from it, too uptight to face whoever was talking to Jessie. The door of the dining-room was open and she went in and sat down, helping herself to freshly prepared toast, pouring tea that had obviously just been made.

'Good! You're up. I wanted to talk to you before I left for the office.' James walked into the room and glanced at her before settling to his breakfast. 'The new guards have arrived for the day. Jessie is just feeding the others and then I'll drive them back to London as I go. The Press are camped outside the gate, so don't leave the estate; in fact it would be a good idea if you didn't leave the house. Jessie assures me that there are ample supplies.'

'I don't think I could face going out today but I can't just stay here and hide. I owe it to my father to face things and...'

'You owe nothing to anyone at all!' he interrupted coldly. 'From now on you make your own decisions. As to going out, give it a couple of days. Before this day is over the City will know who now runs Sanderson-Lyle and they'll not challenge me—I tend to hit back when provoked. I'll issue a statement and share prices will steady, the heat will die out of things and most editors will call off their hounds. Nobody expects you to make an appearance so soon.'

Gemma took a deep, uneasy breath, lifted her fair head and looked directly at him. 'Very well. I'll stay in today. Tomorrow, though, I have to start looking for a flat.'

'You don't *have* to do anything of the sort,' he rasped. 'You have the use of this house and you know that perfectly well!'

'I'm not staying here with you...' she began angrily and he interrupted again, glancing at her sardonically.

'I don't remember suggesting it. I have one mistress already, as you pointed out. For the time being, I'll stay where I belong—in my flat. All you have to do is think straight and eat more than bird seed.'

'I have nothing to think about,' Gemma snapped, colour flooding her pale face, and he stared at her steadily until she was forced to look away.

'I want to marry you,' he said with quiet force. 'All the explanations I care to give were given last night. Until you make your mind up, you have this house. I live in London.'

'I see,' Gemma remarked sarcastically. 'You're offering Brightways as a grace and favour residence?'

'Until I lose patience or you're out of favour,' he growled. 'Meanwhile, you're safe.'

'What do you mean—safe?' Gemma raged. 'I'm beset on all sides. I can't just lurk about here. I have to get a job because I need money, as you perfectly well know. There's Jessie and, of course,' she added scathingly, 'I'll need to buy my bird seed. If you think I'm letting you keep us...'

'I've taken over all the bills for this house for the simple reason that it's now *my* house. Jessie will be paid as usual, by me.' His lips suddenly twisted derisively. 'I'm quite prepared to add to that by keeping you. I can afford you quite easily.'

Gemma jumped up to storm out of the room, embarrassment and a feeling of trembling anxiety flooding right through her, but he was on his feet and at her side before she could even take one step.

'Sit down and eat,' he ordered sternly. 'All this is sheer nonsense and you know it perfectly well.' He was standing looking down at her and she began to tremble even more as his dark eyes held hers. 'I intend to marry you, Gemma,' he said quietly. 'I've fought for what I wanted all my life and it wasn't easy at first. It gets easier with practice, and I've had a lot of that. Now I have everything I want except you. You're the jewel in the crown—a gracious, well-bred wife. When I have you, I'll really know I've arrived. My past will be quite ended.'

'You've arrived already,' Gemma whispered through tremulous lips. 'If you imagine that nowadays you have to prove anything to anybody...'

'Only to myself,' he assured her softly. He straightened up and moved towards the door but stopped to look at her. 'What, in any event, did you intend to do with your life? You have no qualifications. You were never allowed to go to university in case Barry lost you to some young man. You're completely untrained in spite of your intelligence. What can you do other than grace a rich man's house?'

It hit Gemma like a raw whip because it was almost true. The realisation of that flooded over her with frightening speed. Her father had quietly discouraged all her ideas and she had been too devoted to him to offer any defiance. Even so, it was anger at James Sanderson that raced to the top.

'Do you own my car?' she snapped as he made for the door. It annoyed him, apparently, because he turned a very angry look on her.

'I do not own your car! I do not own your clothes or jewellery. The only reason I own anything at all is because your father wanted a deal.'

'And I was part of it!'

'Without you, there would have been no deal at all,' he pointed out menacingly. 'To buy inanimate objects is easy. All you need is money. Buying people is a tricky business, so I never venture into that sort of thing. I want to marry you. I'm prepared to wait—-for a time.'

'Meanwhile, I have a home to live in and no bills to pay?' Gemma enquired, her eyes deepened to dark purple with anger and determination.

'True. For a time, as I said.' He stood looking at her, his eyes narrowed on her annoyed and resolute fate.

'Right!' Gemma stood with her head flung back, two wings of soft apricot anger across her cheeks. Her eyes were glistening with rage, purple and flickering gold. 'Then I'll make a deal, Mr Sanderson—if I can trust you to play fair.'

'My business reputation is above reproach,' he assured her quietly, watching her with unusual intensity, and she knew it was true. James Sanderson only ever needed to give his word, that was well known. 'What kind of deal did you have in mind, Miss Lyle—assuming you have something to deal with other than your beautiful body?'

Gemma blushed deeply but held her ground.

'You think I'm nothing other than a china doll. You say my father treated me that way. Maybe you're right,' she pointed out fiercely. 'You fought your way up by intelligence and hard work. Give me the same chance.'

If it hadn't been so important to her she would have backed down at the look on his face. Fierce speculation, dark intelligence, devastating masculinity that watched her with narrowed, probing eyes.

'Go on.' He was slowly walking back to her and her nerve almost broke. The idea wasn't even formed properly in her head. It was just a stray thought that had surfaced as he had scathingly told her how utterly guileless and useless she was.

'Teach me all about Sanderson-Lyle,' she said a little desperately.

'You have no qualifications.'

'I—I have, in a way. I did a business course and I passed quite well. Daddy didn't know about it until later. H-he thought I was just going out...' Her voice trailed off at the speculative look on his face.

'Deceiving Daddy? Well, well,' he murmured, one dark brow raised. 'And then?'

'He wasn't too pleased. He refused to let me get a job so—so the skills are a bit rusty but I know more than you think.'

He was watching her so intently that she wanted to sink down and get under the table.

'Well then, you have unused, rusty office skills and no experience, except for the gentle art of deceiving Daddy,' he murmured derisively. 'That hardly qualifies you for working with me.'

'I don't want to work with you,' Gemma got out quickly and anxiously, the thought terrifying her. Besides being ruthless and cold he was brilliantly clever, she knew that. He would panic her each day. 'There are plenty of departments, surely—accounts, planning, secretaries...?'

'So?'

'Teach me the business. If—if I can't learn it....'

'If you can't learn it, you'll marry me?' He put his head on one side and regarded her steadily.

'Yes.' Her face paled at the thought, but she had to have something to offer, something to bargain with.

'A deal, Gemma, is a deal,' he pointed out quietly, his eyes still intent on her face. 'If you fail, I'll expect you to keep your end of the bargain.' His hand came out and tilted her face. 'A deal with the devil?' he asked ironically.

'I-I'll keep my word,' Gemma stammered.

'You *will*, angel!' he stated adamantly. He looked into her rather scared eyes for a second and then laughed, that same devastating laugh she had heard last night. 'So you're not all cool and distant after all? Somewhere inside there's a fire burning, even if it's only fuelled by the need to get the better of me. A duel, then, Miss Lyle. Winner takes all.'

'I—I'll need time.'

'Of course I'll give you time,' he assured her with mocking astonishment. 'I'll play strictly fair. It is now the beginning of September. Accounts first, I think. Denzil Price runs his department well and he can teach you—about the business, that is,' he added tauntingly. 'At Christmas we'll assess your progress.'

He turned her mouth up and astonished her by dropping a light kiss on her lips. 'The bargain is sealed,' he murmured, walking off. He stopped at the door, standing to look at her, a dark picture of power, ease and sheer masculine grace. 'If at any time you want to call the bargain off,' he said quietly, 'you can. That goes without saying.'

'And—and if I do?'

'You marry me, of course.' He suddenly grinned at her. 'You grow more interesting by the minute. I detect a sly plan to defeat me. Don't bank on it too much. I'm not easy to vanquish.'

He wasn't. She could still feel that light kiss. It had seemed to burn her, the feeling racing down her arms and tingling in her fingers. All she needed was a breathing space and now she had come up with it. She could stay here at Brightways and make sure that Jessie was comfortable. She doubted her own ability to live in a cheap flat in a run-down district and she just couldn't ask Jessie to face it. Jessie would insist on going with her, though, and she had to make long-drawn-out plans before she moved.

Meanwhile she had this deal and she would work hard at it. It would put her in line for a job with another firm and then Jessie would not have to face hardships, because she intended to win. She was not about to be the pinnacle of James Sanderson's career, a well-bred bride to finally wipe out his poor beginnings.

When she went into the kitchen, Jessie was very busy but looked slightly bemused. The men had gone and she was just clearing their breakfast dishes. For a second she said nothing and then she turned to Gemma with her old determination to have things right out in the open.

'Mr Sanderson told me he'd bought Brightways.' She wasn't asking for confirmation. She took James Sanderson's word without any shadow of doubting. All she was doing was letting Gemma know that she was up to date with events.

'He has. Lock, stock and barrel. Every last scrap of furniture, and I imagine it includes every last pan in the kitchen. As they say in the sales ads, "the contents of the house".'

'Well, it's a relief. It could have gone to a stranger. I love this house.'

'You don't think that Mr Sanderson is strange?' Gemma asked quizzically, and earned herself a look of deep reproach.

'I think he's a gentleman, a fine gentleman. He's strong and caring, no matter what they say in the papers. You can judge the papers by the way they're harassing us now. I don't know what we would have done if Mr Sanderson hadn't been here to protect us. They'll not get past those tough men on the gate. Which reminds me, I'm making them some lunch. One of them will be back for it at about twelve. I never thought last night. I was so upset. They didn't have even a cup of tea all night long.'

'I'll clear the breakfast table,' Gemma murmured, glad of the excuse to go. She had had quite enough of the 'fine gentleman', and didn't even want to hear his name.

'I hear we're staying on here.' Jessie stood with her hands in soapy water and turned her grey head to Gemma, determined to get every last thing said.

'Temporarily.' Gemma edged to the door, feeling her face begin to grow quite hot.

'How long is temporary?'

Well, here it was. She might as well get it over with too.

'Until I tell him quite categorically that I have no intention of marrying him.'

'He's asked you?' Jessie's dour looks suddenly softened to near delight. 'I just *knew* he would one day. I've seen the way he looks at you, even if you haven't. Last night he was really worried about you. He was asking me what you ate and what could I think of to tempt your appetite. When are you going to marry him?'

'Never.' Gemma looked at her firmly. 'I agreed to stay here because we need a breathing space until I can learn office work at the firm and then get myself a better job somewhere else, with more pay.'

'You're *deceiving* him?' Jessie sounded scandalised, she who wouldn't hesitate to lie for her loved ones. It just showed how deep James Sanderson had got himself in her good books.

'He's impossible to deceive,' Gemma said wryly. 'I made a deal—cards on the table. If I can't learn the business, I marry him. He takes it as a sort of duel.'

'He knows you're mad and he's humouring you,' Jessie scoffed angrily, frowning quite ferociously. 'A man like that doesn't need to run after any woman. You'll lose him.'

'I wish I could. I wish I'd never seen him.'

Jessie sniffed maddeningly and turned back to the dishes, throwing one last shot as Gemma walked out of the kitchen.

'I'm getting two daily helps,' she announced importantly. 'Mr Sanderson thinks this house is too much for me at my age.'

'I always help!' Gemma spun round but found herself glaring at Jessie's back.

'He says you're not to. He says you're to relax more. He says you're too uptight. There's two women starting next week. Mr Sanderson thought it best to wait until the Press had moved off the gate. Daily helps tend to gossip.'

For a second Gemma continued to glare, but it didn't get her anywhere. Jessie had imparted her information and gleaned even more. Now she was only the housekeeper again. Gemma stormed off angrily.

Mr Sanderson says this, Mr Sanderson says that! He had said that the Press got in where water couldn't seep. He wasn't so bad at that himself. For two pins she would get out of here and leave Jessie to it. She walked up to her room and had a quick change of heart. From her window she could see the gates. They were locked and the men from the firm were chatting to each other as if they were on holiday. At the other side of the gates, though, there were what appeared to be hordes of people, many with cameras. The Press.

She sighed resignedly. It was only the show of muscle-power at the gate that stopped them coming in and camping right on the doorstep. She hoped that James had his statement issued and that tomorrow would see the back of them. The thought annoyed her even more. How deeply she was in his grasp! How enmeshed. It felt as if some dark net had been thrown over her. For once in her life she had to fight. The alternative was frightening.

CHAPTER THREE

JAMES rang just before it was dark that evening.

'Go up to your room and look out of the window,' he ordered as soon as Gemma answered. 'I imagine you'll be able to see the gates from there.'

'I'm in my room now. What am I looking for?'

'A lack of interest,' he said drily. 'I'll be very much surprised if anyone is hanging around now.'

When Gemma looked, the newsmen were all gone. The men from the firm seemed to be playing cards, and James grunted with satisfaction when she told him.

'I've sent a relief team down to stay the night but after this I doubt very much if anyone will be interested.'

'D-did you issue a statement?' She was nervous just speaking to him on the phone, and she heard that dark laugh that worried her so much.

'Yes. I issued a statement. To the media we are now boringly normal. Even so, I would advise that you avoid looking at the papers for a few days. I did warn you of some colourful speculation. Not everything will have been squashed.'

'Y-you mean about the—the women?'

'Yes.' He suddenly sounded quite grim. 'Understand it and forget it, Gemma. Remember him as you knew him.'

'I do.' It was little more than a whisper, but he heard, and she also heard his quite exasperated sigh.

'Learn to live! You're bright and beautiful.'

'I—I'm going to live. I have to defeat you!'

He began to laugh and to her dismay she could see his face quite clearly in her mind. It brought a strange, uneasy feeling that was almost painful, tingling and twisting along each nerve-end.

'I can accept any challenge,' he assured her. 'If it helps to pull you out of that little shell and into reality, then it's all worthwhile. I intend to win, in any case.'

'So do I.'

'Maybe you'll change your mind about the goal before Christmas,' he derided. 'You do realise that if I'm to teach you about the firm I'll have to see a good deal more of you than previously.'

'You said I could learn from each department!'

'And so you can, but most of the drive comes right from my own office. No point in doing things by halves. When you know enough, you'll be expected to learn to co-ordinate your knowledge. You'll be living right in my pocket each day.'

Gemma was silent. She hadn't thought of that at all, and for a minute he let the silence hang.

'When you're nervous, you stammer a little. Do you know that?' he asked softly. 'Do you want me to come down to Brightways?'

'I do not! You promised to stay in your flat while I was here.'

'Only partially true. I'll stay until we're married.'

'That's not going to happen.'

'Don't sound so frantic, my angel. I'm not about to pounce on you.'

'I can guarantee that. And I'm not your angel!'

'You will be, Gemma. At least, you'll look like one, standing right beside me at Brightways as we welcome our guests.'

She just put the phone down on him because she could see the picture and it was suddenly not as horrifying as it had been. No way was he going to sneak into her life. He was frightening and she hated him anyway.

Gemma didn't start work until the following week. The weather had improved to give a beautiful, warm Indian summer. She spent her time out of doors as much as possible, coming to terms with the truth that she was alone now. She had to face the fact that her father would no longer be there, to coax and tease her, to spoil her and at times to gently bully her—she admitted that last now to herself, although she would never have admitted it to James.

With the advent of two buxom daily helps there was nothing for her to do and she was still nervous of going too far from the house, afraid to meet someone who would bring up the past and rock her new-found calm. She spent much of her time in the garden, soaking in the last of the sunshine, resting and eating whenever she felt able. Gradually, she was recovering, and treacherously her mind asked her if she would have recovered as quickly if James Sanderson had not come so forcefully into her life.

On her first day at work she was more nervous than she had imagined, fully realising that she had so far in her life done nothing to earn her own living. Having been poised and cool for so many years, she had thought she could pull this off without a tremor; but she was wrong. The drive and zest that permeated the whole building made her want to escape and call the whole thing off.

Of course they knew who she was. She had visited here to see her father, but the looks she got now were different, and the feeling in the building, with its great glass doors, its soaring steel and glass shape, was different too. Lyle's had truly gone. She would have known it before but she had resolutely kept away since James had come on the scene. The old, comfortable ways were over. James ruled, his cold brilliance seeming to be in every corridor, every room.

She stood in the vast foyer, irresolute, but not for long. Like a dark magician James appeared and took her firmly in hand, allowing no time for further nerves. He introduced her to the accounts department as if she was just an ordinary employee and his attitude told them all that she might be only Gemma Lyle, not now of great importance to this firm, but that she was quite tightly under his wing. They didn't quibble because they liked her anyway. Many of them had seen her since she was a fair-haired little girl and most of them were sorry for her, she could tell that from their eyes. They knew about her father, of course. The whole city knew. She didn't want pity. She was proving things to both herself and James and she settled down to work with a grim determination that surprised everyone.

She enjoyed it and became utterly absorbed, never noticing the time going by. At lunchtime James came into the office and asked to speak to her, not breaking a rather forbidding silence until they were in the lift and skimming up to his own office.

'I'm taking you to lunch,' he informed her briskly.

'No need. No need at all. I've started to eat.' Having recovered from her nerves, she was now excited about working, buoyed up almost to enthusiasm.

'I assumed so.' His eyes roamed over her until she felt shaken, her euphoria fading fast. 'I noticed the nice little tan and the few added pounds. They suit you. However, that's not the point of the exercise. I'm merely taking you to lunch.'

'Do I have to go?'

His dark brows rose sceptically. 'No. You can kick up a fuss and create a scene if you like. I'm not your father. I don't expect gentle obedience. Fight all you like. I'll still get you in the end.'

'We were talking about lunch, not anything else,' Gemma pointed out, blushing painfully.

'So we were,' he agreed sardonically. 'Have lunch with me, Miss Lyle?'

'If you wish, Mr Sanderson.' Two could play this derision game. Her heart sank when she remembered how little time she had before Christmas. Would he give her longer? What had he meant by an assessment? She watched his dark face anxiously, thinking like mad.

'You spend a lot of time staring at me, Miss Lyle. Do you realise that?' he enquired wryly. 'For the last couple of years it would have been easy to miss if I hadn't been interested in you. Now, though, you seem to float off into some sort of dream-world and gaze at me with terrible concentration. If you want to know anything, just ask. There's no reason to try mind-reading.'

'I was trying to make you disappear,' Gemma said tartly. 'I can see, though, that I've not mastered the art in spite of long nights of study. You're still there.'

He grinned at her impudence, his dark eyes narrowed.

'Better give it up. All the time you're wishing me away, I'm wishing myself closer. I think we're cancelling each other out—the magnet principle. Let me win. We'll both enjoy it more.'

It ensured that she went to lunch with a flushed face, and she hoped the receptionist assumed that he had been telling her off for a poor morning's work. Did she stare at him? She noticed that most of the other women in the building did, and she assumed that he realised it. There was an arrogance about him that belied any poor beginnings. If looks were to be believed, half the women here were head over heels in love with him. Any one of them would have jumped at the chance to marry him, but he stalked like a dark god through their days. He prowled like a dark panther through hers.

She remembered when she had first seen him. Her father had invited him to a large dinner party at Brightways, quite a few months before he had turned his eye on the firm. She had been standing in the hall welcoming guests and she had turned as her father had called to her, a smile still on her face from the words she had been having with old family friends.

'Gemma, darling. There's someone I want you to meet.'

Her father had said that before often enough, and her polite smile of enquiry had simply died on her face as she had looked round to meet the dark, glittering eyes of James Sanderson.

Some dreadful shock had hit her deep inside; her heart had tilted wildly, panic washing over her because she knew right then that this man was not like any other man she had ever met. She saw ruthless determination and a quite deadly interest. She felt threatened, and it was all she could do to place her hand in his.

'Miss Lyle.' He had given a polite half-bow and released her hand at once as he'd felt her instant aversion to him, but she had not been settled all night, and she remembered watching him surreptitiously whenever she could, looking away quickly when the dark eyes met hers.

Yes. She had stared at him, secretly and deeply every time he had come, and she had imagined he didn't know. Well, it was a habit she would have to break. The trouble was, she didn't even know she was doing it.

A hard hand grasped her arm and she was almost lifted on to the pavement, only awakening then to the fact that she had been about to step out into the lunch-hour traffic.

'Don't try to kill yourself,' James murmured ironically, keeping her firmly to his side. 'I need you, Gemma. My car's parked here. I didn't go into the car park this morning.'

'I—I'm sorry. I was thinking.'

'Don't take life too seriously,' he advised, helping her into the Mercedes. 'If you were a bit more light-hearted you might even enjoy yourself.'

'That's difficult. I'm under threat.'

'Wrong. You're being pursued. Haven't you ever been pursued before, Gemma? Hasn't any man told you he wanted you?'

She blushed furiously and looked at her clenched hands.

'I—I've never invited such—such . . .'

'Insolence? Don't stammer. Relax. You're out to lunch.'

She didn't know what to say. He suddenly sounded quite gentle and amused, and she assumed he took her for some sort of idiot. Actually, nobody ever had told her they wanted her before. She was too shy to invite such things, had been too much under her father's protection. She had even had to battle to be allowed to stay out late at first, and any job would not have been countenanced.

'You merely want a well-bred wife and an heir,' she managed in a tight little voice.

'I want *you*,' he assured her darkly. 'I want to look up and know you're mine. I want a lot of things to remember when I'm not at home, too; none of them have to do with social status.'

'You know I won't marry you,' she got out breathlessly.

'I know you don't want to. Time will change that.'

'You're a very arrogant man. You're ruthless and dangerous.'

'Better than being feckless and tardy, surely?' His lip twisted wryly and he glanced at her before starting the car and sweeping out into the heavy traffic. 'Surely you don't expect the same treatment from me that you got from your well-bred boyfriends? I'm leading you along gently, for me—spoiling you. I'm indulging you in the matter of this learning the business although I know quite well it's merely a time-wasting project to put a little distance between us. You don't know what pressure is yet. I'll apply pressure when I feel exasperated enough. Until then you can simply bask in the security.'

'What security? I'm teetering on the edge of a pit!'

'Merely dipping your toes in the water to find out what it would have been like to be free. You never have been free, Gemma. I'm letting you have that freedom for now, but there's security. I'm not about to let you flounder and go under.'

'Why? Why? Why?' Gemma raged quietly. 'Why pick on me?'

'Look in the mirror,' he murmured drily. 'A golden virgin with purple eyes. You're the girl for me. You even shout quietly.' He suddenly grinned and it really infuriated her.

'I see! You want a fast and furious mistress and a weak-kneed wife?'

'Well, it makes for variety. Shall we stop sparring now? We've arrived.'

They had arrived and it was Delgarno's; clearly this wasn't going to be a cheese sandwich affair. It was warm inside, warm and expensive, and for a moment Gemma felt a wave of unease. She had never been here before but the sort of people who came here were the sort of people who knew her father, and she was almost afraid to look round.

'Your table, Mr Sanderson.'

The head waiter appeared and almost fawned on James. Everyone seemed to be looking at them and Gemma felt herself edging closer to him as they walked through the crowded restaurant.

'Relax. Nobody's going to ask you to wash up.' He took her arm firmly, pulling her even closer. 'Chin up, Gemma. Look the world in the face.'

'Even when it's staring at me?'

'Well, I hate to disillusion you, child, but they're staring at me.'

'They've seen your horns?' How she could engage in back-chat when she was trembling she really didn't know, and he gave a soft, dark laugh.

'That's better. No, they haven't seen my horns, they've heard about my latest activities.'

'Me?' Gemma stared up at him anxiously and he looked down at her like the devil he was.

'Such a lack of modesty, Miss Lyle. No. Not you. I've just bought out the Fielding Corporation. It was a bit of a battle. I finalised it last night. The City knows now.' He stood as the waiter helped her into her seat, and then sat opposite, his eyes amused and taunting.

'B-but that's textiles, isn't it? What has that got to do with civil engineering?'

'So. The bird seed didn't damage your brain,' he gibed. 'Yes. It's textiles. I've dabbled in plenty of things since I started, many years ago. Fieldings put up a battle but they lost.'

'Naturally. I wonder you bother with engineering. It's obvious that you're more at home in a fight.'

'Back to the gutter, are we?' he enquired drily. 'I'm an engineer, Miss Lyle. That's why I bother with engineering. It may not be my sole interest but it's my major one, especially now,' he added softly. Sardonic, handsome and suddenly very frighteningly familiar, he leaned back in his chair and looked over the menu. 'Want me to order for you? I know what you like.'

'How can you possibly?'

'You have to remember that, all the time you were staring at me at Brightways, I was watching you, equally interested but not so secretive. I noticed what you enjoyed and what you merely picked at politely.' He suddenly looked up. 'I know you don't care for steak and you adore chicken. You love strawberries but hate the cream. You like champagne, white, dry wine and sweet liqueurs. You always eat your soup and you never spill it on your dress.'

From staring at him in astonishment, suddenly Gemma was laughing, the first time ever that she had laughed when he was anywhere near, and his eyes gleamed with interest, narrowed and dark.

'Laughter lights up your face, makes jewels of your eyes,' he said softly. 'You're a very beautiful girl, Gemma.'

His gaze was so intent that she dropped her eyes in self-defence, nowhere else to hide but inside her own thoughts. But she could still see him even when she closed her eyes and she couldn't escape from the deep, dark voice like black velvet.

'One day you won't be able to hide from me. One day soon I'll know every thought in your mind, every secret in your head, every inch of your body.'

'*Please!* You know I'll never marry you. You know I intend to escape at all costs, even if I have to go away.' She was almost whispering and his hand came out across the table and captured one of hers.

'Don't you mean—run away? Face me, Gemma. Fight back.'

'I—I c-can't.' She raised her fair head and looked at him, and it was quite impossible to look away. She was captured by dark eyes, sinking into the depths. 'Are—are you trying merely to improve my weak character? Stiffen me up?'

He shook his head, smiling and so sure of himself, but he never really answered. All he said was, 'Don't stammer.' It was said quietly, almost gently so that she swallowed nervously and didn't attempt to remove her hand from his.

They had almost finished their meal when Gemma looked up and saw the woman bearing down on their table. It was the only expression she could come up with, and she knew who it was. She had seen Roma Prescott in plenty of magazine articles, even on television, her success a great wonder to the media.

It was no wonder to Gemma. Roma Prescott was driven by the same force that drove James—the will to succeed at all costs. She seemed to be filled with some sort of furious energy; even on television it had come across clearly, and now it crackled around her, drawing eyes to her as she made her way to their table.

It was the same image that Gemma had seen before. The tightly drawn-back black hair, the padded shoulders and tapered trousers, the fiercely blue eyes.

'Darling!' Her energy seemed to explode around them and James looked up with obvious surprise.

'Roma? I had no idea you were dining here.'

'I'm not, darling, but I'll have a coffee with you. It's all I have time for. Order me one, please. I rang your office but they said you were here and I had to tell you that I can make it tonight after all. I was scared you might have made other arrangements,' she added with a look at Gemma that took in every detail of her appearance and then dismissed her as unlikely.

'No other arrangements,' James murmured, signalling the waiter. 'Lucky you arrived, though; I might have asked Gemma.'

He introduced them and the dark, well-shaped brows rose at the mention of Gemma's surname.

'Lyle? Oh, *that* Lyle! I hope you've recovered from the ordeal of it all, Miss Lyle. The Press can be pretty brutal when they get their teeth into a scandal.'

'They never bothered me, Miss Prescott. In fact, I never met one member of the Press. There really is nothing to interest them, in any case.'

'Really? Oh, I know the thing was hushed up, but...'

'Perhaps you could hush up, Roma?' James suggested in a deceptively quiet voice. 'Gemma is still grieving about the loss of her father.'

'But I'm so sorry,' Roma murmured with no sign of remorse at all. 'Having been involved with your father, I expect James is keeping you under his wing for a bit?'

Suddenly Gemma saw red. She didn't like the stress on 'involved'. She liked it even less that Roma Prescott so graciously consented to lending James out for a while. It certainly meant Roma was sure of him. Had he been discussing her with his mistress? Or was this a fishing expedition? Whatever it was she had no right to launch into an attack on her father.

'James *is* looking after me. I just don't know what I would have done without him these past couple of weeks,' she said sweetly. 'In fact, I'm staying in his house. He even makes sure that I eat. You must come down and have dinner with us one night.'

Roma looked unmistakably venomous. She hadn't expected this much protection, obviously, and Gemma saw shock and anger rising immediately, but James just sat back, his lips quirking.

'That's a very good idea. What about tomorrow night, Roma? Come at seven. We'll show you around before dinner.'

He was just enjoying it, Gemma realised. He didn't care any more for Roma Prescott than he did for anything or anyone else.

She glared at him quietly as Roma quickly drank her coffee and left.

'I'm to have Brightways to myself until at least Christmas,' she hissed. 'I never invited you to dinner.'

'You invited Roma. Do you want to tackle her on your own, then? I warn you, you took her by surprise and she was in a hurry, in any case. She'll recover, though. I doubt if you'll get off scot free.'

'I doubt if I'll see her again, so what does it matter?' Gemma snapped.

'Dinner tomorrow night, Miss Lyle, at my house. *You* said it, after all.'

'I hate you more by the minute,' Gemma stated coldly, but he smiled right into her eyes.

'And I want you more by the second,' he rejoined promptly. 'Anger adds interest to an already fascinating subject and, in passing, it's worthwhile to note that you didn't stammer once. Let's remember that.'

'You can't come to dinner!' Gemma informed him tightly, but he just went on smiling, arrogant as the devil and handsome beyond belief.

'I'll be there, though, Gemma. I think I'll stay the night, too. Don't bother to prepare for me, I'll let Jess know.'

'Her name is Jessie!' Gemma snapped.

'She likes to be called Jess. Just try relaxing and you'll find out all sorts of nice things.'

'From you?' Gemma asked scornfully, worried as his smile slowly died, the mockery fading away.

'You know better than that,' he said quietly, his eyes darkly intent. 'I'm not *nice*. Everything I do for you is merely marking time until I own you.'

'Y-you won't own me.' The smiling, almost understanding man had quite gone and Gemma was looking into the face of power and invincibility.

'What do I say to that?' His eyes watched her unwaveringly. 'Maybe it would be best to simply ignore it. You're necessary, part of my plans. Add to that the fact that I want you, and we have inevitability.'

* * *

Gemma wondered later if James would keep to his threat and arrive at Brightways, or if it was all some scheme to undermine her confidence. She should have known better. He was out all the afternoon and all next day too, but, when she got home, Jessie informed her happily that Mr Sanderson was coming for dinner and staying the night. He'd even requested a special menu, and when Jessie reeled it off Gemma recognised a lot of her favourites. She wondered if he would bring champagne just to drive home the point.

He did.

She was just going up to change when he simply walked through the front door, two bottles of champagne in one arm and a bouquet of roses in the other. She stopped on the second step of the stairs and tried her best to look forbidding and haughty. Each time she saw him he affected her more and she didn't quite know how.

'Champagne and roses,' he pointed out mockingly. 'I ordered a bright moon but it wasn't possible to deliver.'

'How disappointing for Miss Prescott,' Gemma murmured sarcastically. 'Never mind, we'll light candles.'

He walked across to her and stood looking up at her as she remained almost poised for flight.

'The roses are for you.'

'Why?' she challenged angrily, annoyed with herself for looking down at him as if he was some sort of wonder. He was so vibrant, the dark eyes holding hers with ease, his sexual magnetism deliberately surrounding her.

'Why? You're my bride-to-be. I know we're not to seriously discuss it for now, but surely I can bring you roses? Notice the discretion. I brought pink instead of red.'

'In case Miss Prescott became suspicious?'

'Because they are more delicate, more befitting to a virgin bride-to-be and, in any case, Roma won't see them, will she? You'll put them in your room. Right by the bed.'

'I'll put them in the dustbin right by the back door!'

'No, you won't angel. You're too soft-hearted.'

She turned and swirled away, going up the stairs fast, knowing he was watching her every inch of the way and knowing she would not throw the roses out either. He knew her just a little too well, even though she had avoided him since she had first met him. He seemed to be able to read her mind.

She didn't know whether to go to dinner in jeans and a sweater to shame him, or dress up to put him in his place. In the end she decided to wear something for the occasion, and of course it had to be black, and she hoped he took the point. She went to a lot of trouble getting ready because she knew deep down what to expect. Roma Prescott's boutiques drew the most wealthy clients. She had built everything up from one small boutique and she looked as if she had walked over plenty of faces to do it. Now there was a chain of them—very exclusive—and she was reported to be very wealthy and equally hard. After meeting her, Gemma had no doubts about that.

She slipped on a black cocktail-dress with boot-lace straps across her creamy shoulders. It showed off her slender figure perfectly and black suited her colouring, the honey-blonde of her hair glittering in the light. She regarded herself solemnly. She felt inexplicably subdued at the thought of James here with his mistress, and the knowledge of that scared her utterly. Why should she bother? With a bit of luck she would be off and free in no time at all.

She was still contemplating her image when there was a tap on her door, and she hoped Jessie hadn't burnt the dinner.

'Come in, Jessie,' she called out quickly, but it was James who opened the door and came inside.

'You can't come in here!' She was stiff with shock. He was invading almost every part of her life.

'You invited me in. I distinctly heard you.'

'I—I thought it was Jessie. Will you please leave now?'

'I brought you something,' he said quietly, walking towards her with his soundless tread like a great, dark cat.

'I don't want it!' She spun away but was just a little too slow. He caught her wrist and held on, swinging her back to face him.

'You don't know what it is. Don't be an idiot, Gemma. I'm not here to seduce you. Just stand still and be good for one minute. I want you to wear this.' Before she could protest he had turned her to face the mirror and was fastening a very beautiful necklace round her neck. It seemed to be amethysts and diamonds in a very old setting, and she just stared at it as he stood behind her and said nothing at all.

'I-I can't accept it. It looks real.'

'It is real. I want you to have it. It brings out the purple in your eyes. I don't know any other girl with purple eyes. I saw it this afternoon and couldn't resist it.'

'Please don't do this to me. You're putting me in a terrible situation,' she pleaded desperately.

'Why am I?' His hands came to her tiny waist as he watched their joined reflections. 'I'm very wealthy, Gemma, and you please me. I want you to wear something I've given you.'

'B-but...I—I...'

He drew her back against him, his hands sliding up her arms, touching the satin skin.

'Don't stammer,' he ordered softly, watching her closely. 'There's no plot, no subterfuge. It's just a necklace.'

'Y-you're wanting to make Miss Prescott jealous,' she said quickly, trying to stem the trembling that had started deep inside, and suddenly fathoming it out. All it did was make him laugh, that dark, soft laugh that she had started listening for.

'No such thing,' he murmured quietly. 'I want to look across and see you wearing something I've given you.' He suddenly dropped a light kiss on her shoulder and then let her go, and she was glad he just walked out of the room because she felt as if his lips had burnt her and that same queer shiver ran over her skin. She just stared at herself in the mirror. Subtly, the necklace had changed her. Before, she had been a well-dressed, demure woman, a girl almost. Now she looked expensive and glamorous.

It took a second to realise that it wasn't just the necklace. There was a glittering look in her eyes and her skin was flushed. She had been tremblingly aware of James, and it just wouldn't do. She hastily put on lipstick and combed her hair again. Somehow she would have to face Roma Prescott. Somehow she would have to face them both. Before it had seemed possible, but right now she felt so vulnerable she could have cried.

Gemma had to admit that Roma Prescott was more glamorous and feminine than she had believed. The projected, driving image was missing. Tonight she wasn't dressed for fashion; she was dressed for James, and looked it.

It made Gemma feel dowdy and quite ill because she had never seen such seductive energy packed into one woman before. The dark hair was loose, swinging around her shoulders, as glossy as her face. She wore a bright red and gold kaftan and her lipstick was an exactly matching red. She had even carried the effect through to the gold eyeshadow, and there wasn't much doubt that this was all deliberate to remind James where he really belonged.

It all seemed to be too much for Jessie, who served the meal and then stayed out as much as possible, but her eyes strayed reprovingly to Gemma when she was in the room, and they spoke volumes. 'Take action or you'll lose him.' It only added to Gemma's anxiety. She felt hopelessly under pressure. Roma's sharp blue eyes watched her for faults and reactions and James hardly ever seemed to look away from her, amusement clearly just below the surface.

'That's a very fine necklace,' Roma suddenly said in a break in the conversation, which was almost entirely her own talk. 'It would probably be worth copying, actually. I can visualise it against a very severe suit.'

'Are you going into jewellery, Roma?' James asked easily—not too interested, if his looks were to be believed. Roma had already pounded him with information, almost ignoring Gemma. She was thinking of starting her own fashion house, designing the clothes herself, adding the few discreet and costly items to her very selective shops.

'Why not, darling? Costume jewellery is the rage, you know. I believe there's a very good return on any capital invested.' She suddenly swung her eyes to Gemma. 'That one looks real. Where did you get it? I could do with a browse through any shop like that.'

It was a very good time to say smartly, 'James gave me it,' but Gemma had now long forgotten the small battle at the restaurant, and the words just wouldn't come. All she wanted was to see the back of both of them and get to bed.

'As a matter of fact, I bought it for Gemma,' James said evenly. 'You may not have noticed but she has purple eyes, very unusual. The necklace does something for her, although I'm not quite sure what.'

'Embarrasses her, I should think,' Roma pointed out, her eyes on Gemma's flushed face. 'What a thing to do, darling. Don't you realise what a position it puts a woman in to have something like that thrust on them?'

'Actually, I didn't thrust it on her at all,' James remarked quietly. 'I simply fastened it around her neck. She understands why.'

'James was my father's friend,' Gemma put in quickly. 'He's h-helping me get back on my feet.'

'Unusually benevolent,' Roma murmured, her eyes like blue glass. 'I've never known him to be so avuncular before, but then, you are a little vulnerable-looking.'

'Feeble,' Gemma said sweetly, furious that they were both regarding her as if she were a freak. Here at her own dinner table! No, it wasn't, not any more. It was James Sanderson's dinner table, silver, crystal and the lot. 'If he's avuncular I expect it's because of the great difference in our ages,' she added, getting one in at him, too.

James merely smiled sardonically, but Roma stiffened for an attack, hearing quite well the sharpness behind the sweetness. After that she barely spoke to Gemma and James did nothing to help out at all. He just sat there looking at her as if she was an idiot that he had decided to improve before he caged her.

CHAPTER FOUR

BY THE time Roma managed to tear herself away at ten o'clock, Gemma was almost ready to scream, and she flatly refused to go to the door politely with their guest. James did, of course, and she couldn't go to bed because they were standing in the hall—murmuring! After one quick glimpse showed her that Roma had her arms wound round his neck she almost fled into the drawing-room, and it was a long time before she heard him coming back into the house.

She expected him to be almost covered in crimson lipstick but he wasn't and he looked at her mutinous face and said nothing.

'I'm going to bed,' she snapped, standing to move past him.

'Does that require any comment? Of course, you might be inviting me, but I doubt it.'

'I can do without remarks like that!' Gemma seethed. 'I've spent a most boring evening and it's tired me more than a fancy-dress ball. I would have thought Miss Prescott would be tired too, all that venom so carefully clothed in ice. Think how weary she'll be tomorrow. I imagine she gets up at five each morning to dive headlong into the day.'

'It's not too far back and she has a lot of energy,' James murmured derisively, giving the whole thing a very erotic slant. 'In any case, she won't take long. She drives a Ferrari.'

Well, of course she did, and she probably had a car phone and a small computer on board. Then she would stride into a space-age bathroom and come out scrubbed and smelling of Givenchy without raising a finger.

'She's not at all pleased about this necklace,' Gemma pointed out hotly.

'Really? I never noticed. It doesn't matter. It will keep her on her toes and guessing. In any case, she'll have no doubts at all where she stands soon. It will be mistress or nothing when I marry you.'

'Pigs might fly!' Gemma seethed, swirling out of the room. It was unbelievable that she was in this situation and she only had herself to blame. She should have simply laughed at him and left straight away. In fact, now that she was recovering from the shock of her father's death she couldn't look back and really understand why she hadn't walked out the very next morning.

Fear, her mind informed her—fear and the inability to face things. James faced things and she had been quite prepared to hide behind him. But it was different now. Jessie was settled here and would stay on, Gemma was sure. She only really had herself to take care of and she could manage quite well. She could sell her jewellery, for one thing. Her mind had been too numb before to think of that.

She undressed and showered and then paced about in her négligé. How much would she get? She went to the wall and moved aside a small Degas print, reaching up to open the little safe there that held all her things. The black velvet boxes laid out on the dressing-table seemed to be like a salvation. The jewellery glittered in the lamplight. There was a lot. Her father had heaped things on her, spoiled her so long as she had been prepared to stay and be exactly what he had wanted.

Tears stung her eyes. It had been bad for both of them, meaning he would never get over the death of her mother and meaning that she had never been free, never faced the world at all. A china doll. She held up a diamond

bracelet, its glitter catching the light. Could she simply
sell these things? Could she get rid of them at all? Every
piece reminded her of some small, happy time in her
life, always with her father, and, in any case, many of
them had been her mother's. She put them back,
defeated.

The evening had upset her more than she had realised;
it had brought home to her that nothing here was hers
at all. Until now she had merely been dreaming in a
familiar atmosphere, but now she saw very clearly that
all this belonged to James. So would she if she didn't
start fighting more, and the thought scared her, especially the feeling it brought.

To be held in those strong arms, to be swept under in
that dark power. The odd flicker of excitement shocked
her even as it rose inside, and she saw Roma Prescott's
sophisticated face. That was what James wanted on a
day-to-day basis. He had fought his way to the top. He
and Roma Prescott spoke the same language. Both were
equally hard and cruel.

It looked as if she wasn't going to be able to sleep,
Gemma decided when midnight came round and she was
still tossing uneasily in bed. Better to get up and break
the circle of restlessness, make a cup of tea. She slid out
of bed and reached for her négligé, hesitating a moment.
It wasn't particularly practical, the satin and lace merely
a flimsy covering over her nightie. Anyway, she had no
intention of waking anyone and there was no doubt that
James would be fast asleep, his mind quite at ease after
his evening spent in tormenting her.

The thought made her tighten her lips in annoyance.
She had never had to fight anyone in her life and she
was angered that she had to now. Not that she was any
worthy opponent, in his opinion; he was merely letting
her wear herself out with the struggle. Well, she wasn't

going to and this evening had definitely stiffened her resolve—not that it had really needed stiffening. She knew what life with James would be like—days of amused contempt, evenings when she would play his hostess, his china doll. Her mind shied away from the nights. The thought of being in his arms made her tremble violently.

It was dark all over the ground floor of the house and she hesitated to put on any lights until she was actually in the kitchen. She managed, with the reflected light from the wall lights of the passage upstairs, and she slid thankfully into the warmth of the kitchen and switched on the light there, feeling she had made it to safety. The whole feeling upset her. She had lived here all her life and there had always been safety.

James had brought danger and unhappiness. She cut off that thought. No, he hadn't. She had been living in a dream-world, a rich girl with nothing to do at all except pretend enjoyment in everyday life. She hadn't particularly enjoyed it. She was too intelligent for the rather vacuous life she had led; often she had been bored and uneasy, feeling she was wasting her life away.

And he had brought a sort of security too, a kind of lifeline to cling to until she could make it on her own. The only thing that marred the picture was his desire to marry her, and she realised that if he had simply told her he would keep an eye on her until she was able to cope she would have been foolishly grateful in spite of her constant feeling of danger when he was there.

The thought was unacceptable too. Was she admitting she couldn't cope? That she needed someone to take over her life as her father had done? That was what James was proposing, after all—security and wealth in exchange for a mindless doll.

She poured a cup of tea and carried it towards the table, her thoughts completely on her own problems, delving more deeply than she had ever done into the reasons for her fear of the dynamic man who now seemed to rule her life. When the door suddenly opened she was shocked out of her deep meditating, jerking round with a wild little cry of fright, and the hot tea spilled over her wrist and hand, making her wince and put the cup down quickly.

'What the hell are you doing now?' James strode across and grabbed her arm, almost dragging her to the sink. 'I should hire a keeper for you and give him a long list of your likely misfortunes!'

'I'm perfectly capable of seeing to myself,' Gemma protested, trying in vain to free her arm. 'And what's more, I'm at liberty to roam wherever I like.'

'With your keeper,' he finished angrily. 'I'm astounded you managed the stairs.' He was holding her arm under the cold tap with a sort of suppressed fury and she struggled uselessly.

'My arm's going numb!'

'To match your head,' he snapped. 'Stop that struggling. The cold water will take the sting out of it.'

'Wonderful! I'll remember that when I'm being treated for frost-bite. This water is icy!'

He just glared at her and let her go, tossing her a towel and then standing back to look at her intently.

'What are you doing, wandering about after midnight?'

'Getting a cup of tea. I couldn't sleep.'

'Now that I can well understand.' Suddenly, his lips twisted wryly. 'You're too old to sleep alone.'

Gemma's face flooded with colour. 'You have no right to speak to me like that.'

'I'm not claiming any rights, just superior understanding. A girl like you should be married by now.'

'Maybe that's true,' she snapped, turning away and making for the door, her tea forgotten in her desire to escape. 'From tomorrow, I'll look out for somebody.' If she had expected sardonic amusement at her little threat she was sadly mistaken. He seemed to almost spring at her, his arms twisting her round and capturing her before she could open the door and escape.

'Start thinking like that and you'll really know what danger is,' he grated. 'If you're casting your eye around the office...'

'As if I would be so stupid!' She was still too annoyed to feel any fear and she still struggled uselessly. He didn't even seem to notice. He was holding her with almost contemptuous ease, his dark eyes burning into her.

'No.' He suddenly relaxed from black anger. 'I would have noticed. I know every move you make. I've known every move you've made for the past two years. I would certainly have spotted a prospective lover.'

'Of course you would,' Gemma mocked angrily. 'Being an experienced one yourself, you'd know at once.'

'I've never pretended to be Sir Galahad.' His grip eased from cruelty and he looked down into her raised and annoyed face. 'I want you, though, Gemma, as I've never wanted anyone. Maybe you're only a dream but I still want to keep the dream, a golden girl drifting down that staircase and right across to me because I own you. I first saw you like that, but then, you wouldn't know, would you? I was there long before your father got around to introducing us. I was part of the crowd of guests in the hall and I saw you. The dream started then. I wanted you to be walking to me, not to one of your suave boyfriends. One day, you will be walking to me.'

His voice had sunk to a low, brooding murmur and she looked into those dark, intent eyes, feeling herself begin to drown. Just for this moment there was no fight in her. She was imagining him watching her without her knowing. Normally the thought would have scared her but now it was exciting, the thought of it changing the look on her face.

'Gemma?' When she stood still and showed no sign of moving he murmured her name, pulling her closer. She was without resistance for now and his hands began to move against her back, soothing and insistent against the satin softness. He had never touched her before like this, never attempted any kind of caress. There had been boys in her life before, and men, but none had ever gone beyond flirting and the odd, snatched kiss, because she had repulsed them carefully.

Now she was spellbound, being drawn closer to a hard, male body that subtly demanded, being stroked by hands that carried their own message. His fingers slid under her hair, massaging her nape, making her feel weak and dizzy and her usual cry came out to ward him off.

'D-don't!'

'I won't hurt you, Gemma.'

His voice was slurred, dark, and for a moment she wanted to go on feeling his touch, the way his hand stroked her neck as his arm tightened slowly around her. He was too intent, though, thrilling danger, his face taut, and with a great effort she sprang away, staring at him with horror, only it wasn't horror of James; it was all directed at herself because she had wanted him to kiss her, had wanted to know just what it would be like when those hard arms closed round her firmly and his lips captured hers. Now she felt as if she had escaped from some terrible danger of her own making.

For a second he watched her, his eyes narrowed, the dazed look changing slowly to sparkling anger.

'You really think I'm a swine, don't you?' he snarled. 'I could be the richest man in the world and you wouldn't even look in my direction. You're tightened up inside like a drum and everything's either black or white. Obviously I come in on the black side.'

'I—it wasn't because...I—I didn't mean...'

'For God's sake stop trembling and go to bed!' He turned away impatiently and she stood looking at him helplessly for a moment before moving to obey. Every taut line of his body was screaming frustration and anger. She was shivering with reaction herself, stunned that for a few mindless seconds she had felt compelled to move to him, to soften.

He was the dark waves of the sea, a storm beneath the ocean, and she would never survive if she gave in at all. She would become a mindless slave while he continued to see women like Roma Prescott. She just fled to her room, locking the door for the first time in her life, and though she lay awake for hours she never heard James come to bed. When she got up next morning he had already gone and for all she knew he had gone the night before, maybe to wake Roma up and seek solace there.

Gemma was surprised how bitter that made her feel, and it only served to stiffen her own intentions. She drove up to London with more resolve than she had ever had, shaking off her tiredness, determined to present a cold face to James.

In the event, he wasn't there at all, and she finally gleaned the news that he had flown out to America without coming into the office at all. Her own disappointment stunned her and she was still in a sort of half-world when she went to lunch.

She chose an old haunt of hers, a small Italian restaurant where she had often come with friends. It was very significant that those friends were now no longer to be seen. She had obeyed James and scrupulously resisted any inclination to look at the papers in the days after her father's death, but she could tell from the angry, scandalised looks that Jessie had maintained then that plenty of things had been written.

There was the firm, for one thing. It was quite obvious that she had lost everything because there had been a lot of speculation in the City when her father died. They had not missed his secret lifestyle either and, though it was less than a seven-day wonder, the words had been written, the thoughts thought, and now she seemed to be very short of friends. There were no invitations to the theatre, no dances. Not that she wanted any, but it simply closed in the net around her more, making her aware that she had James and nobody else at all.

She cursed her stupidity in coming to have lunch in this place when a fair-haired young man walked breezily in soon after her. It was Simon Grainger. At one time he had taken her out quite regularly until he had been posted overseas by his firm. Maybe he had been back long enough to hear the news. She looked down at her plate steadfastly, hoping he wouldn't see her. She didn't want to embarrass him. She liked him and she really didn't want to see his face change when he saw her.

'Gemma?'

He *had* seen her and he came striding across to look down at her.

'What's this? Dining alone? Answer quickly because I'm just about to join you.'

She felt ridiculously grateful to be treated like a human being for a change and not either like a social outcast or a mindless doll, and her smile was warm and welcoming.

'Simon! Oh, do join me. It's ages since I saw you.'

'One year, one week and three days,' he grinned, sitting opposite. 'I'm on leave. I've got two months, less the one week and three days.'

She knew his firm had sent him to Australia and the deep tan he sported was only what she could have expected. It made his crisp fair hair seem fairer still. Even his eyes looked lighter.

'Obviously the life suits you,' she murmured thoughtfully. 'You look...'

'Brash?' He grinned at her. 'Don't let the air of confidence fool you. I always did shake when I saw you. I'm just hanging on to my feelings tightly.'

There was a time when that sort of thing would have embarrassed her, but not any more. The realisation of that made her feel slightly stunned and he noticed the change in her too.

'How are you?' he asked quietly. 'I heard about your father. I'm sorry, Gemma.'

'Perhaps you didn't hear everything,' she suggested softly.

'I think I did. What difference does it make? I liked him, even if he did give me one or two wary looks. I expect he thought I would spirit you off with me one day, not that I didn't want to. How are you managing?'

'I work for the firm.'

It just wasn't in her to tell him that she lived at Brightways and was part of a deal with James. Simon would go on his way and she would never see him again, in all probability. Right now she didn't feel like making up any complicated lies and she certainly wasn't about to tell him why she was still in the security of her old home.

'Work?' He looked suitably stunned and she managed to keep her rising annoyance under control. What could she expect, after all? She had never worked before except in the house as a hostess for her father.

'Well, I wasn't left in luxury.' She said it with a laugh but his face darkened and his hand gripped hers quite fiercely.

'Do you hate it, Gemma?'

'Not at all. I love it. It's a sort of freedom.' It was, she realised. Bit by bit she was beginning to live. Simon found that really amusing and to her relief he dropped the whole subject.

They were talking like old friends when the feeling of being watched grew on Gemma to such an extent that she had to turn her head. It was James with Roma Prescott, and the sight of him when she had been quite sure he was safely at the other side of the Atlantic made her face pale, tightening her up inside until any confidence fled. What was he doing here? Was it a coincidence or had he followed her? She had no idea whether they had been here when she came because she had realised her mistake as soon as she had come here and for the most part she had sat with her head down like some uneasy child.

Simon followed her gaze and grunted with exasperation.

'Still staring at you, is he?'

'Staring?' Gemma turned back and looked into the grey eyes that were now a little annoyed.

'Well, he always did. One of the things that made me furious about coming to any function at Brightways was that Sanderson was always there and always watching you like the proverbial hawk. If you hadn't been so clearly indifferent to him I would have been mad as hell.'

'With what right?' she asked pertly. With James glowering at her and Roma looking pleased as punch, she had the decided inclination to flirt, to show him that he wasn't the only man in her small and petty life.

'No right, just hope,' Simon said quietly, his attractive face softening. 'I was just beginning to think I was making some headway when I was posted away.' His hand came to cover hers on the table. 'It's only for three years, Gemma, and I've already done one of those. I'll be working back in London then.'

'And you'll probably miss Australia,' she put in quickly. She didn't know what he was leading up to but immediately she was uneasy, the habits of a lifetime springing to her aid.

'I thought you looked different but I can see you're not,' he acknowledged with a wry smile. 'Still the same old Gemma, holding people off with both hands. Let's compromise,' he added, looking at her quizzically. 'While I'm here, go out with me. If you don't hate it, who knows what might happen?'

She would probably have refused but she looked up and saw James deep in conversation with his lady love, his smile so very obviously that of a lover, and a small attack of silent rage forced all inhibitions away.

'I'd like that,' she said quietly, smiling into his eyes. 'Actually, I missed you, Simon.'

The effect on him was remarkable and she had instant qualms about what she was doing but it was a little too late now and she only hoped he wasn't seriously attracted to her. He escorted her out of the restaurant and into a taxi with a very proprietorial air that made her more uneasy still.

'I'll ring you tomorrow at work,' he promised and before she could stop him he grabbed her quite firmly and kissed her startled mouth.

When the taxi drew up outside the Sanderson-Lyle building, the silver Mercedes drew up behind and James was out of it before she could even pay the fare. James did that and dismissed the taxi with a curt nod.

'Get in the car,' he snapped, taking her arm with the usual firm grip.

'I should be back at my desk. I...'

'You should be doing as you're told,' he rasped, pushing her into the warm luxury of the car and getting in beside her. 'The boss is right here and, if anyone questions you, tell them that. Who was your lunchtime companion?' he continued without so much as a pause for breath.

'An old friend and I don't see what...'

'No old friends, Gemma!' He turned her to face him, hard fingers on her chin. 'I'm letting you have plenty of time, plenty of rope, but men friends were never part of the deal. You're marrying me. Competition is out!'

'I am not marrying you. Simon and I have known each other for years. I was going out with him regularly before he was posted to Australia.'

'Yes, I remember. I was trying to place him. Grainger, isn't it? I knew you were going out with him more than anyone else. I didn't like it then and I like it less now. Drop him or he'll find himself posted to the moon!'

'You have no authority over Simon.'

'I have a considerable clout in the business world and plenty of people need favours. Drop him or he can repack his bags.'

'Y-you c-can't do this to me...'

'I can and I will. I'm letting you play for a while but you're mine and don't forget it.' He suddenly pulled her forwards and covered her mouth with his own, kissing her with a hard determination that had her struggling weakly. It was over in a second but she felt the possessive rage, the iron determination, and she was dazed as he opened the door and let her out.

'I'm going to the States,' he informed her coldly. 'Concentrate on this game you're playing and forget Grainger, because I'll be back.'

With that threatening statement he simply drove off into the traffic and she stood on trembling legs and watched him go. Suddenly she was not at all sure if she was going to come out the winner in all this. What was supposed to happen at Christmas after all? One thing was sure; she had to be away from here then and quite secure, Jessie taken care of. How had she got herself into this mess?

*   *   *

A month later, Gemma found herself ordered to work with James. He was remote and cold, behaving as if there was no sort of secret between them, no sort of deal at all. She had driven herself hard and James had wanted constant reports on her progress until everyone in the gleaming offices knew that either Gemma Lyle was destined for great things or she was being punished.

Of course, nobody said anything at all, but there was a great deal of quiet sympathy that warmed her. Nothing about James warmed her. Since returning from America he had been strict and icy, speaking to her when necessary and ignoring her at other times, and in the month she had worked in two departments.

The summons to his office brought a chill of apprehension, especially as he was talking on the phone when she went in and merely motioned her to a seat without even glancing at her. She found herself watching him as usual, the way his dark hair tried its best to wave but was strictly groomed into place. The way his eyes were shielded by thick, long lashes. He was making rapid notes as he listened and he seemed to have forgotten about her altogether.

'You're moving up here,' he announced abruptly, finishing and throwing his pen down on the desk.

'I'm not ready.'

Her shaken reply seemed to infuriate him but he kept his annoyance to his eyes and his tightly controlled voice.

'I'm ready,' he snapped. 'I want you where I can see you and, if this game is to be played according to the rules, then I'd better start teaching you what happens here. From tomorrow you'll be my personal assistant.'

She almost gaped at him.

'Me?' It was something she had never even thought of. It was probably beyond her capabilities. 'I—I wouldn't know how to start. I—I've only been...' He stood with an impatient movement and it was almost impossible to imagine that he really wanted to marry her. He was just the boss, very decidedly the boss, her file in his hand.

He glanced down at the papers he slid to the desk.

'You've been very good in each department and I'm not at all suggesting that you're now an accountant or anything else. Apparently your typing's good and you can use a word processor.' He glanced up with a sort of bafflement on his face that quite amused her out of terror. 'I had no idea how far this business course had taken you. I had never even imagined you could type.'

'I took extra lessons with typing and the word processor. I took lessons for ages. My father didn't know about that either.'

James's eyes narrowed at this admission and for a minute he simply looked at her, but he made no comment about it. He just tossed down the file and leaned against the desk, looking down at her as she sat on the edge of the seat like some office junior being interviewed.

'You wanted a chance,' he reminded her. 'You wanted to learn the business and I promised to play fair. I'm keeping my end of the bargain. Let's see how you manage as my personal assistant.'

'What will I have to do?' It was exciting and also a bit alarming. She had never been given responsibility before in her life and also she was uneasy about this 'playing fair' bit. She wasn't sure he would consider she had been playing fair if he knew she had been going out regularly with Simon during the time James had spent in America. She was supposed to be having lunch with Simon today, actually, and it wasn't going to be easy if she was under the eagle eye.

'What will you have to do? Why, everything, Miss Lyle. Be assured, you'll earn your keep. If things get too rough don't forget that I once offered to keep you.'

There was a knock and Archie Swift put his head around the door, his presence allowing Gemma to escape from the taunting dark eyes.

'Can I see you, James?' It was obvious he was worried and James nodded and then turned to Gemma.

'There's an office already cleared out for you, first on the left after mine,' he said briskly. 'Move in there now. I'll see you later.'

She just had time to nod to Archie Swift and then she got out fast. Archie Swift was the engineer from one of the sites and she knew from his face that there was some sort of trouble. It gave her a breathing space to think this one out.

A personal assistant! If she could pull this off she would be able to get a job away from here quite easily. Personal assistant to the managing director would look very good on any application form. She wondered if James would give her any sort of reference? Well, he had promised to play fair. Somehow, though, she didn't think he would count that part of the deal. Still, it was interesting, and if she could just get control of her shaking limbs she would be able to do it, she was sure.

She didn't even have time for her morning coffee. She was just settling herself in and sipping her drink when the intercom buzzed and James said coldly, 'Bring your coffee in here, Gemma.' She didn't. She just abandoned it and went in at once, rather surprised to see Archie Swift still there, both of them poring over blueprints.

'Trouble at the Westfield Block,' James growled as she came into the room. 'We're going there now. You're coming with us.'

He was referring to the vast office-block they were building, and she knew it would be like ice out there in November. She had to get in touch with Simon, too, to cancel her date if they would be out for long.

'I'll get my coat,' she murmured obediently, getting herself a suspicious look from James and a sympathetic look from Archie.

'It's cold there,' he conceded with a rueful smile and an odd look at James.

'She can wrap up warm,' James murmured dismissively, adding as she made for the door, 'Bring a clip-board. You can take notes.'

She knew from the look on Archie's face that this was utterly unnecessary, and could only conclude that she had annoyed James in some way and he was punishing her by trying to freeze her. She dived for the phone as soon as she was in what was now her own office.

'Simon, I can't meet you for lunch,' she announced breathlessly as he came on the phone.

'Oh, I see. You've gone off me, have you?' he challenged in amusement. There was a rather possessive indulgence there that gave her pause for thought, but she hadn't time to take it up with him.

'It's just that I have to go out to one of the sites.'

'What? It's freezing, Gemma. What the hell are you going out for at all? You're not an engineer and you're certainly not one of the construction workers.'

'I'm a personal assistant,' Gemma snapped. 'I've been promoted.'

'Whose personal assistant?' he asked with a very quiet tone that should have warned her.

'Why, James, of course.' She didn't know there was a sort of singing to her voice, a sort of excitement, but he heard it and at the other end of the phone the rather boyish face clouded with anger.

'What's his game?' he snapped. 'You'll never be a personal assistant if you live to be ninety.'

She was quite stunned for a minute. This was now not normal for her. In the time she had been with James her own self-image had changed and she had never even realised it. Simon was talking about her as if she were some sort of social butterfly without a working part to her brain.

'I know more than you think,' she informed him crossly. 'Anyway, I didn't call to tell you that. I phoned to let you know I have to cancel our date.'

'Gemma, I'm sorry. I know I've annoyed you and I didn't mean . . .'

'I'll get in touch with you later,' she said hastily, realising he had kept her talking for far too long. 'Goodbye, Simon.'

When she put the phone down, James was standing in the doorway and his face was like black thunder but, frighteningly, he didn't say a word. When she slipped her coat on and picked up her clip-board and her bag he simply glared at her and advised her to bring a scarf. After that she found herself trying to keep up with him on the way to the lift.

It was bitterly cold on the site and Gemma reflected that there was something about mud and deep, rain-filled holes that attracted biting winds. She huddled in her coat and followed James, dutifully popping her hard hat on her head when he collected his and handed hers across. It didn't keep her warm but it was regulation.

She took notes when he snapped orders to her. She was used to his cold efficiency but at the moment he was completely harsh and she supposed he was annoyed about Simon. After a while he seemed to let her just slip from his mind and she knew she was no use here whatever. He was simply showing her that she would never be anything but what he had intended for her—his hostess and the mother of his child.

The thought gave her a curious pain inside and she couldn't really bear to look at James at all because she kept seeing a dark-haired child with deep brown eyes. It shook her utterly, twisting her up inside, and she wandered away, not wanting to be close enough to see him because it was beginning to hurt her in a strange sort of way—bitter-sweet.

Later she could only think that it was the cold and her own numbed feelings that made her so careless. She wasn't really looking where she was going, her mind no longer interested in following James and learning the business in order to defeat him. She was simply thinking about him very deeply. When a plank across tarpaulin presented itself she stepped on to it, and even then not too carefully.

She heard a shout—more than one, in fact—and the world seemed to take a great leap sideways as she found herself slipping, the plank tilting giddily. It was impossible to save herself and she fell—a long way down into a trench.

CHAPTER FIVE

For a moment Gemma was stunned, unable to move, lying on her back in wet mud, utterly surrounded by it, her eyes watching James in a dazed way as he slid over the edge and came down to her, his beautiful suit as covered in mud as she was herself.

'Are you all right?' He simply knelt in the wet, his hands raising her head, the brown muddy water running from her hair. 'Gemma! Did you bang your head? Did you hurt your back?'

It was only then that she noticed the length of the trench, the heavy pipes laid end to end. By some miracle she had fallen to the side—a few feet more and she could have killed herself. Her face paled even further and she shook her head.

'I—I'm all right. I—I missed them.' It was pitiful how weak she felt and she gave in to a desire for comfort and buried her face against his damp jacket, not caring whether he liked it or not.

'Get a ladder over here!' James called up impatiently to where men stood and looked down at them worriedly. 'She seems to be all right but we could do with getting out of this damned trench.'

He was holding her very tightly and she was too stunned to help much as he carefully got her to the top. She seemed incapable of doing anything but cling to him, and it was only as he got her to his car, his coat wrapped around her, that she came to her senses enough to realise that James was white with more than shock. He was furious.

'What about...?' Archie came up and leaned to look in at the window, his own problem unsolved.

'Do as you damned well like!' James snapped and then shrugged angrily. 'Oh, what the hell, I'll try to get back.'

He drove off and Gemma dared not ask where they were going. She had committed the ultimate sin of carelessness and James would no doubt tell her so without much mercy when he was sure she was uninjured.

He drove straight off and after a second she found the breath and the courage to ask where they were going.

'My flat,' he snapped. 'It's either that or the local hospital. If you're all right I can get back to work.'

It worried her but she knew it was sensible and she couldn't seem to stop shaking. She was wet, muddy and miserable, and James was hardly in a state to go back to the office. They both looked as if they had been in a war zone.

He ushered her inside when they arrived and she was glad that few people were about. This was a very upmarket area and the residents were not accustomed to seeing two bedraggled people entering such luxurious abodes. She knew it was luxurious even though she was hardly in a fit condition to look around. The whole place seemed to breathe wealth.

'Get a shower,' he ordered tersely as she stood and dripped muddy water on the polished floor of the hall. 'There's a guest-room; I'll shower in my own bathroom.'

He was angry, simply indicating which door to use, and she walked off, staggering a little, still shocked and dazed.

'Can you manage?' he asked tightly. 'Is anything hurting you?' He came forward quickly and held her arms, turning her.

'I can manage.' Her eyes refused to meet his. If anything was badly hurt it was her pride, and she knew she was going to hurt more when he finally decided she was fit to be lectured. It had made her feel inadequate. She was ridiculously hurt by his attitude. He would have had more concern for a stranger. It was a miracle she hadn't been killed, and he was as forbidding as if she had deliberately walked into danger to annoy him. She didn't know why his lack of concern should hurt so much, but it did.

She looked up at him, her eyes miserable as they met his and his face tightened even further, his grip on her arms actually hurting.

'Look, just get your shower and then...' His voice stopped as she went on looking at him unhappily, and he muttered under his breath.

'Oh, hell! What am I going to do with you?' He picked her up, carrying her to the guest-room, standing her in the bathroom as he turned on the shower. She was too numb to realise it when he took off her jacket and draped it over the edge of the bath. It was only as his fingers came to the buttons of her blouse that she came to life.

'James!' Her pale face flushed and her tragic looks turned to sheer reprimand.

'What am I supposed to do, stand here and let you shiver?'

'I—I can manage.'

'Call me if you can't.' He hesitated for a moment as if he was undecided whether or not to leave her, but finally he turned and left and for a few seconds Gemma was too listless to move.

She moved finally, though, and stood in the shower letting the warm water flood over her, trying to scrub herself clean, washing her heavy hair until it was once more the colour of honey. There were a couple of bruises on her face and she had grazed her leg, but by and large she had had a very lucky escape and she knew it. She felt badly shaken, shivers running over her skin from time to time, even though it was perfectly warm in the flat. And she hadn't a thing to wear!

Gemma looked round in dismay as this disastrous thought came to her. Her wet and dirty clothes were in a heap on the floor, and short of a trip to a cleaners she was left with nothing at all. Her tights and undies were splattered with the mud from everything else. She washed them out and then went to the door.

'James?'

Opening the door a crack, Gemma shouted to him, but got no answer at all so she wrapped a towel around her and went to the bathroom door to call again. He came in so quickly that she felt dizzy.

'What's the matter?'

He was already showered, clean and shining, his dark hair still damp. He was wearing another suit but he had only got as far as putting on the trousers and his shoes. His shirt was unfastened, open to the waist, and at the sight of him Gemma felt in a turmoil. She stepped back, clutching the towel, a shakiness inside her that was nothing to do with her fall.

'I—I'm all right. It—it's just that I haven't a thing to wear.'

She couldn't seem to take her eyes from the rippling muscles, the smooth, tanned skin, the way dark hair arrowed downwards to his belt. He was wonderfully tall, she thought, his height intimidating when she was barefoot and only covered in a towel. Colour flooded into her face when she realised he was simply watching her intently, and she couldn't meet his gaze.

'I hadn't forgotten about that little problem.' He stared at her thoughtfully, his eyes on her flushed face. 'I'll get your clothes cleaned. It doesn't much matter for now because you're staying. While you were showering I made the bed up for you in here.'

She noticed then and it made her feel trapped, ridiculously vulnerable. She had wild visions of being here all night, sleeping next to the room that James occupied, and her face flooded with more tell-tale colour as she imagined him sleeping, his skin brown against white sheets.

'I want to leave.' Her voice was tight with tension and he advanced like a marauding tiger, slowly and dangerously.

'You're going to bed! You've had a considerable shock and though I think you can manage without a doctor there's no way you're going to stride back into a busy day.'

'I know how I feel. You're not trapping me here!' She felt lost and if she didn't fight him she had no idea what else to do. She found herself wanting to touch him, to let her hands run over that brown skin, and it scared her. She had never wanted to touch a man before in her life.

'Trapping you? You could have killed yourself today with no trouble at all. If that's all the sense you've got, then we'd better call this deal off and announce the wedding.' His cold voice brought her back to reality, back to the dangerous thoughts she was allowing to creep into her mind.

'There isn't going to be a wedding. When I get married it won't be to you!' Because she was scared of her own feelings Gemma was shouting and she knew it, backing away as if he threatened her, and he looked furious at the way she so plainly rejected him.

'You're planning on marrying Grainger?' he asked scathingly. 'Better reconsider. He doesn't earn enough to buy your earrings.'

It stopped her in her tracks. It was perfectly clear what he thought of her. It had always been perfectly clear, after all. She was a useless creature who needed a man with plenty of money and asked for nothing else. She wasn't dynamic and successful like Roma Prescott. She was a useless rich girl, now poor. She flew at him, forgetting her scanty covering and her previous embarrassment.

Right in front of her eyes she could see the same face that had smiled at Roma Prescott so coaxingly and he was looking at her as if she were utterly stupid and frivolous. She wanted to wipe the scorn from his face, to claw at him, and her reaction took him by surprise.

She was upon him before he expected it and only his swift action in capturing her in hard arms saved him from the blows she now aimed at his chest.

'Put me down!'

He was holding her so that her feet were no longer touching the ground and she was crushed to his chest, her legs kicking and her hands beating at him. All thoughts of keeping the towel securely round her were gone.

'I hate you! I've always hated you!' There were tears stinging her eyes, gathering at the back of her throat, and he heard them. He let her slide to the floor, keeping her securely at bay.

'Stop it, Gemma!' he ordered. 'You've had a nasty fall and a shock. This is not doing you any good at all.'

'Nothing will do me any good. I'm leaving, do you hear me? I'm leaving this flat and then I'm leaving the firm. I don't know why I made this stupid deal. Jessie doesn't need me. I can get a flat. I can sell my jewellery. I don't need *you*!'

She burst into tears, clutching the towel to her, bending over as if she was heartbroken. She could almost hear him comparing this childish outburst to Roma's sophistication and she was bitterly ashamed that she had let herself slip like this. He made her feel hopeless and it was getting worse. Never before in her life had she let her cool poise be shattered. All she was doing was proving to him what he already thought, and now it seemed to matter very much what he thought.

He muttered under his breath and swung her up into his arms, cradling her for a minute, and she was too shaken and aching to struggle, tears sliding down her face.

'Let go, Gemma,' he said tightly. 'Stop fighting everything.'

'It has to be me, doesn't it?' she sobbed and his lips twisted in a bitter way.

'Maybe it's me. I know you hate me. If I had any sense I'd let you go. Unfortunately I don't seem to be able to. I want you for myself any way I can get you. Roll out of that wet towel and snuggle down.'

He put her on the bed and she managed to struggle free of the towel and still keep herself decently covered. Tears were still choking her and she closed her eyes tightly, the sheets pulled to her neck as he dropped the towel on a chair and turned back to her.

'What's this? Cowardice? Don't you care to go on shouting at me?' When she opened her eyes he was standing looking down at her. 'Let's get back to that fall. Tell me where you hurt.'

'All over.' She tried to close her eyes again but he tilted her chin and forced her to look at him.

'Where particularly?'

'There's no special place. I'm just shocked, I think. Th-that's why I...'

'That's why you felt the need to remind me how you hate me? I know.' He still went on looking down at her and she was filled with a wild agitation. All her antagonism seemed to be seeping away.

'I'm grateful to you for what you've done,' she said shakily. 'You didn't need to take care of me, make this deal... I'm no concern of yours and...'

'But you are, Gemma. I'm going to marry you.' He sat down on the bed, close to her. 'I think it's time we talked about it.'

'There's nothing to talk about.' She would have liked to move away but she was very much aware of the fact that beneath the sheets she was naked and each small movement she made seemed to bring his eyes to her body. 'Can't you just go and get my things cleaned? Can't you go back to the site and—and...?'

'Leave you? No, I can't. It's time you woke up, Gemma, and I'm going to be the one to wake you. Maybe if I'd had a different beginning I could have watched you date Grainger and smiled benignly. Maybe I could have played the stupid games his type plays.' He let his hand rest lightly on her breast through the covering of the sheet, ignoring her gasp of shock. 'I didn't have a different beginning, though; I fought for what I wanted. Now I want you.'

He kept perfectly still, his dark eyes holding hers, hypnotising her, and Gemma knew she should be pushing his hand away, defending herself, but the thoughts were momentary, floating like swirling leaves at the top of her mind. They sank and were dragged under as desire, sharp and sweet, burst like a flood, engulfing her.

'You like this?' He was watching her intently, noting every change in her expression. Her eyes were darkened, like black pansies, the purple almost gone, and he moved his hand coaxingly, a mere flexing of warm fingers. It brought a flare of soft colour to her cheeks and her tongue moistened her parched lips with an almost secret movement that his eyes followed hungrily.

'Does Grainger touch you? Do you let him hold you, kiss you?'

Warning voices whispered in her mind, telling her to assure him that Simon was much closer to her than James ever suspected. Thoughts of resistance, self-protection dimly came but quickly went. His hand was softly moulding her breast, his other hand stroking back her hair, and her lips parted in a sort of mute appeal that had him reaching to lift her up into his arms.

She felt the hard warmth of them close round her, the softness of his shirt against her bare skin, and within seconds she was pliant in his arms, melting, no thought of resistance in her head at all.

'You're mine, Gemma,' he said deeply. 'I want you soon. I'm tired of this game.'

His power overwhelmed her until she seemed to be drowning in velvet darkness, her face tilted for his kiss, unaware that her mouth was moving convulsively under his, her fingers in the thick gloss of his hair. She was arching towards him, letting him draw her closer and closer, and she hardly heard him speak.

'Let me look at you.'

His voice was low, husky, a compulsive command, but she had become soft, being in his arms, submitting fatalistically, oblivious to anything but the arms that held her and the kisses she craved. Maybe she had always craved them? Maybe that was what all the fear had been about?

James drew the sheet away, slowly uncovering her with a look on his face that was almost reverence, and she moaned frantically as his dark head bent and he took one rose-tipped nipple into the warmth of his mouth. Her fingers tightened on his shoulders and he looked up at her and then shrugged out of his shirt, tossing it aside.

'Touch me!' he ordered huskily. 'Touch me, Gemma!'

She didn't know how to begin but he lifted her close again until her breasts were crushed against his bare chest, the peaks aroused and aching as he moved her against him. His hand slid down her back, his fingers tracing every bone in her spine until she gasped and melted into him, her hands feverishly moving over his smooth brown shoulders and the strong column of his neck.

It seemed to fire something deep inside him because he pulled away the sheet altogether and turned her into his arms as he came down beside her, kissing her urgently, deeply, making her almost drowsy with feeling. His fingers stroked her, his hands exploring her body, desire crackling from his fingertips, and she moaned against his lips.

She murmured anxiously but he merely deepened the kiss further, his arm sliding beneath her, lifting her closer, his hand under her hair, cradling her head. She felt dizzy, everything swimming, a burning feeling flooding through her that started at her toes and washed completely over her body.

Sensation drowned her and she gave no thought at all to where this was leading. It was like a drug, something she needed, and she clung to him urgently, moving where his hands led, her lips fused with his, refusing to be parted.

'Do you want me to take you now?' he murmured deeply, his teeth biting gently and insistently at her silken shoulder. It merely heightened the fire in her. She was impatient, lost in desire. She wanted to feel all his skin against hers, not just the smooth, muscled hardness of his chest. She wanted to know what it would be like to belong to him.

Unknowingly her hand moved to his waist, her slender fingers sliding inside the waistband, and he gasped harshly, tightening her to him so that not an inch of space separated them.

'Is that an answer?' He tilted her face, speaking huskily against her mouth. 'Do you want me to stay here with you, make you mine completely?'

'Yes! Yes!'

She had forgotten everything—who she was, what he was, her future and her self-respect. All she could do was feel and ache, tormentedly seek for something she had never even known. Her trembling eagerness seemed to snap his last control and he rolled away, pulling her on top of him, moulding her against him as his powerful body moved explicitly beneath her.

'God! I want to,' he muttered raggedly. 'You're hurt and shocked and not even in full possession of your own mind at this minute, but I want to take you.'

She placed her trembling hands at each side of his face, urgently seeking the lips she seemed to need so badly.

'James!'

'No!' He rejected the plea in her voice, turning her back to the cool sheets and looking down at her. 'I haven't forgotten what you think of me, Gemma. There's no way you're going to tell me tomorrow that I seduced you when you were too shaken to resist. When I take you you're going to be one hundred per cent fit, with your eyes wide open.' He looked down at her, his hand running possessively over her nakedness, his dark eyes burning at the aroused passion of her breasts. 'At least you know now what it will be like.'

He moved and she grasped his hand, his name a shaken sob in her throat, and his eyes moved back to hers.

'I know,' he said thickly. 'You're hurting. Marry me, Gemma, and you won't hurt any more.'

She would. It would hurt every minute because James had made no bones about the fact that he wanted her for all the wrong reasons. He would be with her when he wasn't with Roma or some other woman. When he tired of her she would be just what he saw—a useless china doll. She pulled the sheets over her and turned her face away, ashamed as she had never been in her life.

'It's too late, angel,' he murmured harshly. 'I know what you look like and I know how you feel.'

'You don't,' she managed huskily. 'An experienced man could do that to anyone.'

'And more,' he finished derisively. He stood and collected his shirt, putting it on and standing fastening the buttons, looking down at her as she steadfastly kept her eyes tightly shut. 'Better open your eyes,' he added in sudden amusement. 'You've got to face me some time and it may as well be now. Are you going to still be there with your eyes closed when I bring your clothes back?'

She opened sparkling eyes and glared at him, her face flushed deeply.

'I probably won't be here. I expect Miss Prescott leaves things of hers here from time to time. When you've gone, I'll borrow them and get a taxi.'

He just laughed down into her flushed face.

'You can search by all means. Look in every drawer, every cupboard. For each garment you find, I'll give you a hundred pounds.'

'Only that?' she snapped furiously. 'I can see you're mean as well as unpleasant.'

'Marry me and I'll give you everything. Any dream you have, I'll make come true.'

'How could you? I'll be dreaming of Simon.'

He looked so angry that she clutched the sheets around her with a sudden surge of fear, and it was enough to stop whatever retaliation he had planned.

'I don't think so,' he murmured sardonically. 'From now on you'll be dreaming of what nearly happened here.' His eyes narrowed intently. 'If I thought for one moment that Grainger had done more than tentatively hold your hand you would most certainly not be lying there giving me any back-chat.'

He walked out of the room and she flung herself off the bed, dragging the top sheet with her and wrapping it around her, starting to search the drawers with furious energy. She had to get out of here and she couldn't very well leave in wet undies and nothing else.

James walked back in, standing fastening his tie and watching her with exasperated amusement.

'Save yourself the trouble,' he suggested. 'There's nothing here for a girl to wear and in any case you're having a quick nap, remember?'

'I don't need one and I don't need . . .' Gemma spun round, forgetting the length and cumbersome quality of the sheet. It seemed to wrap itself round her legs and she slid to the floor in an ungainly heap, making his eyebrows rise in astonishment.

'I'm never quite sure whether you're mad or not,' he muttered, striding forward and lifting her up. Before she could stop him he had deftly unwound the sheet and turned to make up the bed again.

'Stop it!' She looked round frantically for the wet towel and managed to get it round her before he turned to her grimly. He advanced on her determinedly when she tried to back away.

'Don't you touch me!'

'Only as a keeper,' he assured her. 'Medicinal purposes only.'

Before she could put up any good resistance, he had whipped the towel away and lifted her into his arms, dropping her on the bed and slapping her lightly on the bottom as she scrambled to get the sheet round her. It was so familiar, like—like a lover, and she looked up at him with wide eyes, forgetting to be furious for a second.

He looked down at her quizzically and then his lips twisted with a wry sort of regret.

'I'm sorry,' he murmured. 'Not about the slap,' he added as she looked astonished. 'I'm sorry I made you go to the site. I should have had more damned sense. It was cold and unpleasant and I didn't need you there.'

'Then why did you make me go?' He was standing finishing dressing, fixing his tie, putting his jacket on, just as if they were married, she thought, scared at the warm feeling it gave her.

'So you couldn't keep your lunchtime date. Pathetic, isn't it?' He shot her a wry smile. 'I suppose that makes me worse than ever?'

He didn't wait for a reply. He just walked out, giving orders on the way as usual.

'Go to sleep for a while. I plugged a phone in by the bed. I'll ring you in good time before I collect you. I've no idea how long these instant dry cleaning people take.'

Once again she had this overwhelming feeling of familiarity, as if she had known him all her life, as if she knew him better than she had ever known anyone. He paused at the door and she stared at him anxiously. He was wearing a deep grey suit, his blue shirt and striped tie perfect, and she found herself realising yet again that he always looked superb. He was handsome, a tall, lithe figure that needed no words of praise. She wondered if he knew how he looked, his dark hair carelessly immaculate, his hands powerful and graceful. Yes, he probably did. There was arrogance about him, no sign of gentleness. If he was ever gentle to her she would be lost forever.

She looked away hastily, her face flushing uncomfortably.

'Sleep.' He looked at her for another second and then left. She heard the door close quietly as he left the flat and then she was all alone with her thoughts. She could do without any of them. She turned on her side and closed her eyes, faintly surprised to feel herself dropping into a curiously relaxing sleep. She could still feel his arms around her, the taste of his kisses on her lips. Her breasts were still alert and slightly painful but oddly enough she felt no sort of regret, only shivers of excitement and a warmth she had never known before.

She must never fall in love with him. It was the last thought she had as she went to sleep.

He never encouraged her to feel anything but annoyance and tiredness; she felt plenty of that. As far as James was concerned the incident at his flat might never have happened because neither by word nor look did he let it surface. For the next week or so he was only intent on the office and the sites so that she soon began to feel that maybe she had imagined it all. Only her feeling of anxious excitement when her eyes met his assured her it had been real. To James it had meant nothing at all apart from a momentary desire, and the thought both angered and dismayed her.

Even so, she was well aware that the days to Christmas were rapidly dwindling, and her eyes were constantly drawn to the calendar on his desk when she was forced to work with James. Jessie was not helping either. She was already beginning to fuss about the festive season, remarking that it wouldn't be the same without Mr Lyle, and pointing out that there would now be no friends to fill the house.

'What friends?' Gemma asked bitterly during one of these mournful sessions. 'They disappeared as soon as they knew there was no money. I can do without such friends.'

'Well, Christmas is going to hit us badly. Maybe Mr Sanderson will join us?' Jessie said hopefully.

'He'll have other plans. In any case, I'll probably stay in London and go out with Simon. He returns to Australia straight after Christmas.'

'That leaves me, I suppose?' Jessie sniffed, and Gemma was filled with remorse.

'Oh, I'm sorry, Jessie. You know I wouldn't go off and leave you. We'll have a Christmas by ourselves. When it gets a bit nearer we'll arrange it.'

Certainly the prospects seemed a bit grim and, if it hadn't been for Jessie, Gemma would have gone off somewhere until the holiday was over. She had other worries too. At Christmas there was to be a reckoning, an assessment. She worked like a slave at the office, listening intently to everything James said, and following his orders to the letter.

She was still seeing Simon but she had never invited him to Brightways. She saw him at lunchtimes when she could get away from James, and sometimes she stayed late in London and went to a show with him. It wasn't pleasing him very much.

'Why don't I come down to Brightways for the weekend?' he asked one lunchtime when she hastily looked at the clock and gathered her bag. 'You're working like mad and I only see you in brief spells. A weekend together would be good for us. It would bring things to a head.'

It certainly would—if James found out. He never came to the house and she knew his weekends were completely taken up with Roma, but it didn't mean he would not suddenly appear. It was his house, after all. Then again, Jessie would most probably pass on the information by accident or design when he eventually appeared. No, it was just too risky and, truth to tell, she would feel somehow treacherous if she invited Simon for the weekend.

'I can't invite you, Simon,' she said uneasily. 'It's just not possible.'

'Why not? You imagine I'd attack you?' he asked a trifle testily. 'I've never attacked you yet and you're not without a chaperon of unnerving qualities. I expect Jessie is still there?'

'Yes, she is, but it's not that at all. You know I wouldn't think anything like that about you.'

'Maybe you'd be more interested in me if you did,' he said huffily. 'All right, I'll drive down and have lunch with you on Saturday. We'll go out from there.'

'I can't.' Gemma saw his face begin to almost freeze and she had to tell him. It was no use putting it off any longer. She should have mentioned it at first but she had never imagined he would be so persistent about going out with her. Now it seemed like a state secret she was about to impart.

'I can't invite you because the house isn't mine,' she said as steadily as she could, keeping it all on an even keel.

'What do you mean, not yours? You're living there!'

'Only until Christmas. James bought the house. He—he's letting me stay there for the moment.'

'With him?' Simon looked ready to explode and she quickly explained, or tried to.

'Of course not. James lives in London. He—he bought the house when Daddy died and because I had nowhere to go he—he let me stay. After Christmas, things will be different.'

It was as far as she was prepared to go with explanations, and she suddenly felt very relieved that she hadn't still got a load of friends hanging around. She would have had to gather them all together and explain *en masse*, she thought hysterically, imagining it.

'Let me get this straight,' Simon said angrily. 'You're living at Brightways for now, thanks to Sanderson's generosity, but after Christmas the generosity runs out. Is that it?'

'More or less. It was good of him, after all,' she began hastily. 'I'll be able to have a flat of my own then and...'

'A flat? After that great house? How did he get it from you? Some neat trick, I imagine.'

'He arranged it with my father. It had to go, Simon, and James wanted it. He's always wanted it, apparently.'

'I bet he has—and you!'

'Of course he hasn't. Don't be silly.' She flushed as she realised how often nowadays she seemed to be telling lies, small and great.

'Silly? I'm a man, Gemma. I know when somebody is eating you up with his eyes, and Sanderson has been doing it for two years, to my knowledge.'

'You must be wrong,' she managed with a shaky laugh. 'I think it's something about his eyes. They're unusual and—and anyway, he has a habit of looking straight at people.'

'No doubt with his arrogance,' Simon snapped. 'I've never noticed his unusual eyes undressing anyone else, though.'

'I wish you wouldn't talk like that. Look, I'll have to go. I'm late for work.' Gemma stood and edged away. He looked furious and she was at a loss as to what to do. She felt like telling him it was nothing to do with him, but, after all, she had encouraged him to think she wanted to go out with him so regularly and she'd known all the time it was simply to keep her mind off James and her other problems. Now she seemed to have landed herself in a mess.

James wasn't too pleased when she got back, either. She was almost half an hour late and she felt his eyes on her as she came across the foyer and went to the lift. He was just going to the lift himself and he glanced at his watch.

'Rather a long lunch-break, Miss Lyle. I imagine you're trying to annoy me.'

'I'm not. I couldn't get away.'

'You were being held too tightly?' He seemed to tower over her in the confined space of the lift. 'I seem to remember telling you to drop that particular admirer.'

'Well, I didn't choose to obey!' Gemma turned on him, refusing to be intimidated. 'And it's no use trying threats because his leave is almost up.'

'Who's threatening? I can afford to be lenient. We're almost there.'

'Where?' She looked at him anxiously as the lift stopped at their floor, and he smiled down at her with dark, sardonic eyes.

'Christmas, Miss Lyle. We assess your progress then, I believe.'

It sounded very ominous and Gemma was glad to get to her room and have a minute before she had to face him again. She still didn't know what was going to happen at Christmas.

CHAPTER SIX

GEMMA hadn't really come round from that when James rang for her, and when she went in he was looking at her with a mixture of anger and exasperation on his face.

'You're really learning, aren't you?' he asked abruptly, leaning against his desk and staring at her disconcertingly. 'I thought butter wouldn't melt in your mouth at one time but I'm discovering new traits every day. First I find that you go wild in my arms and beg to be possessed. Now I find you're very devious.'

She didn't know about devious, but his remarks about her in his arms were enough to silence her completely, and he looked at her for a moment before saying, 'I just had a phone call from your admirer. As I understand it, I'm a fiend who robbed you of your home and who is going to throw you out at Christmas.'

'Simon! He—he rang you?' She just stood looking astonished, especially as he seemed to be amused when he should have been furious and probably was, deep down.

'You have other admirers I don't know about?' he enquired mockingly. 'In this case, it was Grainger. Apparently he's not about to let you be tossed out into the cold, homeless and weeping. He's going to marry you and take you back to Australia with him.' His lips quirked at her woebegone face. 'No need to worry. I assured him of your probable survival. I also refused the offer on your behalf. Clearly he hadn't got the whole picture. I told him he wouldn't be able to marry you, as you would be marrying me.'

'I—I w-won't be.'

He just reached out for her, pulling her close.

'You mean you're just prepared to live with me? I intend to marry you. I refuse to be just your lover.'

'You won't be anything.' She struggled but he simply held her firmly, slowly drawing her closer. 'After Christmas I'll be leaving.' Gemma flung up her head, refusing to avoid his eyes. She had done enough of that already and it had got her nowhere at all. 'Jessie doesn't need me any more. I'm free to do as I choose.'

For a second his hand tightened in anger but he controlled it and looked down at her imperiously.

'You're not free, Gemma. You know that, so just admit it.' His fingers came to stroke down her cheek. 'You've changed, my pet. You've partially come to life and you want me. It alters things in my favour.'

'I do not w-want you!'

'No?' He caught her to him, his lips crushing hers, his arms tightening until she could feel the power of his stomach pressed against the quivering softness of her own. It was possession, and a wave of feeling hit her like a sheet of flame. Her arms slowly moved around his neck, clinging to him in submission, and his knee moved impatiently to part her legs and move her closer. She could feel the triumph in him but it didn't seem to matter any more. She wanted to be here, close to James.

'I like you better with no clothes,' he muttered against her mouth. 'I'm not waiting for you much longer, Gemma.'

The hard, probing evidence of his desire throbbed against her and her hips seemed to move of their own accord to accommodate him until he grasped her soft curves with harsh intensity and pulled her to lean completely against him. His mouth was open, consuming, and Gemma moved where he led, not a thought in her mind but the searing pressure of his kisses and the hard demands of his body.

His hands slid over her intimately, moulding her breasts and stroking her slender thighs until she tightened her arms around his neck and gave herself up to pleasure and excitement.

'How much more of this do you think I can take?' he demanded hoarsely, tilting her flushed face to his. 'You're not a child. You know what you're doing to me. Marry me now! Stop hiding away from me. If you want to go on working, then for God's sake do it, but marry me before I go mad for you!'

Gemma had no idea of what she would have said. She was so filled with desire, so enraptured that at that moment she would have promised anything. She never had the chance. The door opened without so much as a knock and Roma Prescott was there, looking at them with amused eyes that held a flare of rage at the back of mockery.

'James, darling! Honestly, do you ever stop? I never realised you took your expertise into the office, and with your little protégée, too! Is this part of your recovery plan for her?'

Gemma felt James stiffen with anger but he was very slow to let her move from him and he refused to let her move away completely. She could still feel the urgency of his body and, even now, his fingers brushed her breast. He could face Roma with astonishing ease but he couldn't let Gemma go. Desire was still crackling between them.

'Try making an appointment next time you want to see me, Roma,' he suggested smoothly. 'That way you won't be shocked.'

'I'm not shocked, darling. I know you have a succession of lady friends. This one seems to be a bit tame, though.'

'She's not tame enough,' James said brutally. 'She refuses to marry me. I'm persuading her.'

It was like seeing a statue crumble. Gemma was unable to move, still breathless from his kisses, still aware of his hands on her, and the energy and drive in Roma seemed to fade before her eyes. For a moment she stared in disbelief and then turned to the door, her face white with anger.

'Give in, Miss Lyle, do,' she bit out. 'He always gets what he wants. He's never wanted to marry any of them before. I really can't believe he's going to settle down, so there must be a plan somewhere. Better watch out. He never does anything for no reason.'

The door slammed and Gemma found she was trembling from head to foot, staring at James as if he was the worst kind of villain. It was a look he interpreted with ease and his anger grew by the second.

'Why did you tell her that?' she whispered, pulling away from him.

'Why not? It's the truth.' He shot her an angry look and walked back round his desk, putting some distance between them. 'Don't imagine she'll spread the glad tidings. Roma plays a deep game of her own and she's more persistent than most.'

'I don't care what she tells anyone,' Gemma managed in a trembling voice. 'I'm not going to marry you.'

'Time will tell,' he snapped. 'Pretty soon I'll get tired of waiting for wedding-bells. A few moments ago they were the last thing in my mind. We both know what's going to happen. Get the hell out of here, Gemma, before I decide to start all over again!'

Apparently James was prepared to wait until Christmas in spite of his threats, because he didn't push his advantage further. He even relaxed into some sort of normality until Gemma was lulled into a quiet state of waiting. Since the first time she had seen him there had been a feeling of tension whenever he was near, and now she admitted that it had not gone away when he had left.

He had been a frequent visitor to Brightways and between his visits she had often thought about him, more than she had been prepared to admit. There had been a sort of destiny about her feeling for James. The dark eyes had watched her, his presence dominating her as if he had her at the end of an invisible line and was just waiting to pull her in. Now she understood why and she also understood her underlying fear of him. He had wanted her and inside she had known it. She had wanted him too, but she had been too inexperienced and controlled to either realise or admit it.

Now he suddenly became the boss and, in some peculiar way, a friend. She was also proud of herself, something she had never been in her life. She was his personal assistant and more and more work was being delegated to her. Only now did she understand how much she had learnt while she had been here and how good James was at teaching. He had planned her every move and for the first time in her life she was *somebody*. She had no illusions about it. There would have been no way that she could have risen so rapidly in any other firm. She was here because James wanted her close to him, but she was doing the job and doing it well. She had surprised him. His narrow-eyed looks when she coped told her that.

It gave her a feeling of glee and her face brightened, her eyes sparkled. She pored over plans and details with James and felt completely at ease. It was only on the odd occasion when their eyes met that any feeling of desire was allowed to surface but James squashed that immediately, turning away or breaking the sudden silence with some caustic remark about the personnel that had her grinning to herself. He was a great boss. She had to admit it.

Simon didn't get in touch with her again. He had apparently decided that she had been utterly deceitful, and, though it left her with a guilty feeling, she was glad when she realised he would already have gone back to Australia. Roma didn't come into the office again either, but Gemma hadn't much doubt that James would be seeing her. The prospect of a wife in the offing wouldn't at all put Miss Prescott off her stride.

James announced that he would be going out of the office on Friday, and left her a variety of orders that she was now well able to cope with. What she couldn't cope with was the feeling of disappointment that she wouldn't see him for the rest of the day and that meant not seeing him until Monday.

'I'm going to look at that new stretch of road off the motorway,' he informed her. 'If they take much longer we'll be breaking our contract. They need a shot in the arm.'

There wasn't much doubt that they would get one if James was going in person. She just nodded and then looked uneasily away. She had been staring at him intently, wanting to keep him in her mind until she saw him again.

'If anything happens, let me know,' he finished, after looking at her for a few minutes as she kept her head turned away.

'Anything like what?' Gemma asked, meeting his steady gaze by gathering her courage firmly around her.

'One never knows,' he murmured mockingly. 'We're living in interesting times, after all.'

He turned to go and Gemma went back to her obsessive watching. He seemed to be letting his hair grow a bit longer nowadays. It was funny. However late he worked he never looked tired. It was this invincibility, she supposed. What would it be like to be married to him, to welcome him home, to talk things over in front of the fire?

He turned back quickly to look at her, his dark eyes glittering as he caught the expression on her face.

'If you're not careful, you'll get to like me,' he warned softly. 'Added to desire, that could prove to be a problem.' She just gazed at him, colour flooding into her face, and he added quietly, 'Don't forget who's the boss when I'm out.'

Gemma stared at the closed door. Did he mean that *she* was the boss while he was out? Did he now trust her that much? It was true that she intercepted all phone calls and smoothed his days tremendously. It was also true that he was leaving more and more work to her. She couldn't do a single thing without checking with James, but people were asking her opinion now. Until she had been with James nobody had asked her opinion in her life. Jessie ran the house and her father ran everything else.

Of course, she had planned the dinner parties and seen to it that everything ran smoothly, but it was only what she had always done. If the truth were known she would have been better off taking a job as a housekeeper than coming here. But James had taught her and she had learned fast, and she knew it was not just her determination to get the better of him. It was, more than anything else, his praise that she wanted.

She *was* getting to like him; more than liking, she was almost daring to love him, and added to desire it most certainly was a problem. It was a problem that she would keep very much to herself, though. James must never even suspect. The thought depressed her. Things could not go on as they were doing, with James keeping strict control of his desires. Besides, she was beginning to feel almost ill when he wasn't there.

By Monday, Gemma was pale and listless, a small, niggling pain inside that kept her in a state of discomfort all the time. It had been there on and off since her father's death, and she had put it down to nerves, but now she began to suspect that it was nothing to do with her mind at all. Maybe it was the fall at the site, a pulled muscle? Whatever it was she felt pretty grim, but she made it to work and settled down to the day.

James wasn't there and there was no message. It wasn't long before the phone calls began to come in thick and fast and Gemma was earning her keep with a vengeance.

He came in at ten and the only reason she knew he had arrived was that he cut in to one of her calls and took over. It annoyed her out of all sense of proportion and she knew perfectly well why. She had wanted him to call to see her first. She felt left out of his life, deprived. It was ridiculous.

When he sauntered into her office she sat tight and pale, right back where they had started, and all because of jealousy. She wanted to ask him where he had been, why he was late. Instead she took refuge behind her cool poise.

'I'll take you to lunch,' he offered when she looked up and then quickly looked away.

'I'm not very hungry, thank you.'

'What's wrong with you?' He moved from leaning elegantly by the door and walked across to her desk, looking down at her intently.

'Nothing at all. I've been very busy this morning. The phone never stopped and...'

'And you resented being thrown in at the deep end? I had things to do.'

'I'm sure you're the boss and don't have to explain yourself to anyone,' Gemma managed in a tight little voice. After longing for him to come, she now wanted him to go because she felt more in pain than ever.

'So you're angry with me,' he murmured with every sign of satisfaction. 'Come out to lunch like a good girl and I'll make it up to you.'

'You're treating me like an idiot!' Gemma snapped angrily, and his flashing gaze lanced over her in amusement.

'What else do you imagine you are, sweetheart?'

The ironical tone silenced her, that and his words. He hadn't called her that before. She wanted him to call her nice things, and all it meant to him was light mockery. A shudder ran over her and he noticed.

'Are you all right? You're pale again. Tell me what's wrong.'

'Absolutely nothing.'

'Gemma!' The harsh warning note had her looking up and his hand came out swiftly to tilt her face and keep it turned to him. 'I'll take you down to see the doctor. He's in this morning.'

'Look! Just leave me alone! I know how I feel and I'm not going anywhere. You can't treat me like a fool one minute and then...then...'

'Make love to you the next?' he finished roughly. 'I want to look after you.'

'Why?' It was her turn to ask the unexpected question, a trick she was learning from James, and his face darkened, his eyes skimming her pale face.

'Because... Hell! Suit yourself! I'm never short of a lunchtime companion anyway.' He just released her and walked out, and as far as Gemma was concerned that was the end of the day, because she didn't see him again.

He seemed to be deliberately keeping out of her way and by Friday she was resigned to it. One of the many calls she answered was from Roma. So it wasn't ended. It was like a terrible desolation. Suddenly there seemed to be nothing to look forward to any more.

When James unexpectedly walked in at the end of that day he stopped suddenly and looked intently at Gemma, coming into her office and closing the door.

'What's wrong?' he demanded. 'No putting me off this time, Gemma. I haven't seen you for a couple of days and you look ghastly.'

'Surely you don't imagine it's because I'm missing you?' she murmured derisively, wanting to lash out at him.

'I have no such illusions,' he bit out. 'I'm well aware that in the normal course of events you wouldn't even look in my direction. I'm taking advantage of your insecurity, what did you expect?'

His harshness made her more pale than ever.

'You're white as a sheet.' He came to stand over her. 'I'll take you home.'

'No! I'm perfectly all right.' She was so anxious that she found herself snapping at him again and his face tightened from concern to annoyance.

'Very well,' he said stiffly. 'I'm not prepared to make an issue of it, but one thing at least I can insist on, being the boss. You leave now. Right this minute.'

She stood and began to collect her things, but he never moved, his eyes fixed intently on her white face. She winced with pain and he was up to her in two steps.

'Forget it,' he snapped. 'You'll go in my car, and if you argue,' he added furiously when her head came up defiantly, 'I'll carry you to the lift and across the foyer to the car park. Argue your way out of that, Miss Lyle!'

'My car!'

'Damn your car! I've warned you.'

Knowing he was quite capable of anything, Gemma didn't try to argue at all and when he held the door open for her she simply went meekly, glad to be facing the comfort of his car because she suddenly felt she might not actually make it back alone.

The pain just increased. All the way home she was silent, fighting the waves of pain that washed over her, their severity growing with each attack. James said nothing but the speed of the car increased, and as they came into the hall at Brightways he called for Jessie and ordered Gemma to bed.

She was glad to go. For once she was prepared to ignore his domination. How she could be feeling like this she had no idea. She was struggling with her clothes, having to sit on the bed to do it, when Jessie came in to help.

'Doctor's on his way,' she announced, looking at Gemma anxiously. 'I can't understand how you've got like this. I thought you were looking healthy and happy under Mr Sanderson's care.'

Gemma ignored the carelessly tossed-in praise of James.

'Doctor? I don't need a doctor. You had no business to call him, Jessie. He's going to think I'm a complete fool, calling him out here for a bit of tummy ache.'

'Mr Sanderson called him,' Jessie informed her huffily, 'and, if you ask me, it's a good job he's here. Even if it is only tummy ache it might be food poisoning, you being so sick too.'

Gemma was about to point out that as she hadn't had any lunch, and as the last meal she had eaten had been breakfast, here, then if she was poisoned Jessie was to blame. She never got the chance to make any such remarks, however, because she was staggering off to the bathroom to be sick again and after that she felt too weak to argue.

'Hospital,' the doctor said as he stood after examining her. 'Appendicitis, my dear.' He had been the family doctor since Gemma was a little girl and she knew him very well. He wasn't a man to fuss. Jessie fussed,

wringing her hands and murmuring until James came
and firmly took control.

'I can get her to hospital before you can get an am-
bulance here,' he said tersely and the doctor gave one
of his wry little grimaces.

'The anxious fiancé,' he murmured, not knowing
James and mistaking the situation. 'There's not all that
much of a hurry, although I want her there as quickly
as possible. She's a woman, my dear chap. She'll need
time to collect half a ton of luggage to take with her.'

Gemma found herself glaring at him, her white face
relaxing a bit as she discovered that James was doing
the self-same thing. He wasn't used to being told off as
if he were a boy. Their eyes met and he suddenly grinned
at her, making her heart leap. He never grinned like that.
It was a sort of secret look that passed between them
and for one second they were in exact accord.

'Pack her trunk, Jess,' he ordered. 'I'm taking her,'
he added to the doctor, who looked him in the eye and
simply gave in. It made Gemma feel a bit smug. This
particular doctor had always been a bit of a bully,
scathing too. It paid him back for the times he had been
here and looked at her as if she were useless.

'No arguments?' James murmured as the doctor left
to alert the hospital.

'No. I don't like him. It gives me great satisfaction to
see him put in his place.'

'Then we're in complete agreement,' James assured
her. 'I object to being called an anxious fiancé.'

'I'm sorry about that. It's just that he doesn't know
you.'

'Don't get too sorry. I only objected to the anxious
bit. I expected him to start calling me "laddie". That
would have been too much.' He reached for her dressing-
gown. 'Let's get you moving.'

'Th-thank you for—for...'

'Bossing you about?' he asked. 'I intend to go on doing it. It's all good practice.'

'James. I can't marry you,' she murmured tearfully, having to lean on him as fresh pain washed over her. He swung her up into his arms, treating her very carefully, keeping his voice low.

'If you don't, you'll end up living with me and we both know it, Gemma. That little icy surface has cracked. You've had your first taste of freedom and it's done you good. You're a real woman now.'

'Am I?' She had to rest her head on his shoulder as he carried her down the stairs.

'One hell of a woman,' he muttered. 'I'll explain it to you after Christmas.'

'Feeling woozy still?' The sister looked down at Gemma and smiled in a very professional manner. 'It will wear off. These little operations are nothing nowadays, no pain at all.'

Gemma wanted to ask her if *she* had had her appendix removed recently, but thought better of it; Sister looked as kindly as a computer and there would surely be reprisals. She managed a brief smile and Sister went so far as to pat her hand.

'That's better. No self-pity on my ward, Miss Lyle. The anaesthetic does tend to linger with some people. It was very late last night when you had your operation. By lunchtime you'll be raring to go.'

She walked off briskly, disgustingly healthy, and Gemma watched her wryly, wondering if she would be expected to polish the floor before tea. She gave a subdued little giggle and even that hurt.

Gemma turned her head on the pillow, her face twisting in pain. They had told her that she hadn't got in a moment too soon. Left any longer it could have been a much more serious operation. As it was, she would be out of here in just over a week. And then what? Two weeks to Christmas. Already there was a bustle in the hospital, the nurses excited. They were trimming up for the event; she had seen that as she had been wheeled to the theatre.

She would be off work for a few weeks and during that time Christmas would have come and gone. She didn't know how she would face it without her father. Somehow they had always made something of it, although the time had brought grief too, the spirit of her mother always seeming to be there, her father often dropping into silent, black moods that he had struggled out of.

They had filled the house with people and lived through it. For the last two Christmases, James had come, and Gemma moved uneasily in her bed when she remembered how she had resented it, how coolly she had received the gifts he had brought, how she had wilfully never given him one.

What was she thinking of? He was never short of company. She knew, and had known then, of the sophisticated parties he attended, with glamorous women. Getting on better with him was one thing, being maudlin was another. She wondered what he was doing now? It was Saturday, the office closed. Her mind went to his flat, imagining him there, but she cut off the thoughts quickly as Roma Prescott insinuated herself into the scene.

A stab of pain that was mixed with anger hit her more severely than any operation. She was jealous! It couldn't even be thought of. Some woman would always be there, he had almost made that clear.

She was just drifting into sleep after lunch when James came in. It wasn't visiting time, but she couldn't think off-hand of anyone who would be capable of stopping him in any action he had decided on. This was a ward with three beds only and at the moment she was the only patient there. Even so, he glanced round in irritation and then walked over to her, looking down at her intently.

'How do you feel?'

'All right. According to Sister it doesn't hurt a bit.'

His lips quirked in amusement and he sat down on the bed close to her. 'They told me a week and then a good long rest.'

'You enquired, of course?' Gemma looked up at him half resentfully, feeling her utter vulnerability, and he simply nodded, giving her a wry look.

'Now who's to take care of you if I don't? Left to yourself you would have ended up with an emergency operation.'

It made her feel guilty but before she could get out any thanks or apologies he changed the subject.

'What are you doing about Christmas?'

As it was the thing that had been occupying her mind before he came, she looked at him a bit warily. 'Resting, I suppose. Jessie and I were going to try for some sort of festivity, but now it would be a bit difficult. I imagine we'll have big fires and some sort of dinner.'

'Spend Christmas with me.'

Gemma glanced up quickly, surprised to see a look on his face that was almost pleading. It went so quickly that she might have imagined it, but just for a minute it had been there and it stopped any quick retort.

'I—I don't imagine I'll be really up to any parties... I can't leave Jessie, and anyway...'

'And anyway you can think of much better things to do than seeing me,' he finished for her.

'I wasn't going to say that. You just took me by surprise.'

'Did I?' He got up and began to pace around, suddenly impatient. 'God! I wish Christmas had never been invented. The last two years it's been bearable—coming to Brightways.'

'It was a miserable time for us,' Gemma murmured, not exactly knowing what to say. 'We missed my mother. But you—you surely spent Christmas at every party going?'

'So I did,' he muttered. 'Counting the time when I could decently visit Brightways again without too obviously forcing myself into the place.'

'I—I didn't know you liked the house that much,' Gemma said awkwardly. 'No wonder you were happy to buy it.'

'I wanted to see *you*!' He swung back to her with an almost savage look that changed to quizzical amusement when she looked back at him a little wild-eyed. 'I'm obsessive about you, Gemma. Didn't you know?'

Her pale cheeks flooded with soft colour.

'I'm sure Miss Prescott would have been only too willing to...'

'Oh, stop it, for God's sake!' He came and sat on the bed again, taking her hand. 'I wanted you the moment I saw you. It doesn't take much for a dream to turn into an obsession. Behaving like a teenager doesn't exactly suit me,' he finished with a grimace.

'James...'

'Don't say no before you've thought about it, Gemma. I'm not asking you to spend Christmas at my flat. Before you came so coolly into my life I used to fly out to Bermuda to get away from it all. My aunt has a villa there. You'd like her. She was my mother's sister. She can't live in England because of the climate. Come with me and recuperate there. Jessie can come too.'

'I—I can't. What will people think?'

'Whatever they damned well like. What people are we talking about? Your friends?'

'They seem to have faded away,' Gemma murmured ruefully. 'But even so...'

'Gemma!' His hand tightened on hers and she suddenly knew she was going to give in, even if it was only so she could see him more often. Roma Prescott wouldn't be there, anyway.

'I'll ask Jessie.'

'Then you're as good as there,' he pointed out with a smile, his shoulders relaxing. 'I've got her right under my thumb.'

'We'll see about that,' Gemma said mutinously, trying to keep the smile off her face, and he looked right into her eyes, lifting her hand to place it against his lips.

'What does it matter? When we're married she can take care of both of us.' He stood and moved to the door. 'I'll arrange the tickets.'

'I haven't said I'll go,' she began, but he looked back at her in amusement.

'You've given me a big enough hint. You're weakening. The time to get to you is when you're ill and in bed, nowhere to run to. I'm learning all the time.'

The sister came in as he was leaving, losing her brisk, healthy image, her efficient face flushing with coyness.

'Ah, Sister.' James smiled at her in that way he had, making the colour in her face deepen. 'I want Miss Lyle moved to a private room. Things were in a bit of a rush last night. However, I dealt with the paperwork as I came in today.'

'I'll stay here!' Gemma said as loudly as she could, the huge breath she had to take hurting her badly. She had to cling on to some sort of lifeline before James swept her under totally.

'Please move her as soon as possible, Sister.'

'I'll deal with it at once, Mr Sanderson.'

They were talking about her as if she weren't there, and Gemma could see that James had tightened the reins even further when she had left just one chink in her armour. He wouldn't order Roma around and dismiss her wishes so imperiously.

Gemma moved impatiently, forgetting her operation in her sudden annoyance. Tears sprang into her eyes and she bit down hard on her lip, not quite stifling the moan of pain.

Dark eyes flashed to her, narrowed and then turned on the sister with acute authority.

'Miss Lyle is in pain, Sister. I see no cause for that in these enlightened times.'

'Why, no. I'll get her something immediately.'

'You're very kind.' It had the sound of a subdued threat, a tiger purring, and he went out, not looking back at Gemma at all. He didn't need to hang around to see that his orders would be carried out. His orders were always carried out and Gemma faced the sister's now grim face; evidently she had heard the threat too, and Gemma was certain that retribution would follow. Probably the needle instead of a tablet. She wondered if she should just give in to James? She was beginning to feel utterly miserable when he wasn't there.

'Is Mr Sanderson your fiancé?' Sister asked somewhat grimly.

'In a peculiar sort of way,' Gemma agreed wearily. In a peculiar sort of way he was, she supposed. He intended to marry her. He ordered her about. Only the ring was missing, and she was beginning to think that the one in her nose was already there.

CHAPTER SEVEN

GEMMA flew out to Bermuda with James two days before Christmas. Jessie had agreed enthusiastically to the trip when James had taken Gemma home, and there had been no way she could get out of it after that. Later, though, with a volte-face that left Gemma stunned, Jessie declared herself to be too wary and far too sensible to fly. She announced her decision to spend Christmas with her married brother, and from the way she talked about it Gemma could see it had all been planned from the moment she had heard about Bermuda.

'You knew you were going to do this!' she accused, and Jessie met her shocked annoyance with a bland face.

'I never get to see my brother. I wasn't going to go off and leave you alone; I never have done, have I? And another thing,' she added primly, 'I hear from Mr Sanderson that his aunt Hester is his only relative. It's time you met her, as you're going to be one of the family.'

'I am not going to be one of the family!' Gemma retorted, but as James had driven up at that moment she had to put up with Jessie's disbelieving sniff and let it go. James merely said it was unfortunate, but his amused looks told Gemma that he had expected it all along. Maybe he had even planned it with Jessie. It seemed that everyone was quite free to follow their inclinations—except her.

Now, as she sat beside James, she mused about how he had changed her life. She had been cold and withdrawn, quite sure of her hatred and fear of him. It seemed now that her fear was about her own feelings. She was getting used to being swept up into his life.

She knew he was ruthless and had settled on her with a fixed determination. She knew all about his affairs and she knew most certainly that he didn't love her at all. It seemed to be inevitable, though. They were drawn together by an almost unwilling attraction and they both knew it.

She glanced across at him and he was looking at her with triumph gleaming in his eyes. It had been there since they had boarded the plane, a deep excitement in him that had swept around her almost tangibly. For a week she would be with him all the time.

'How are you feeling?' He looked at her possessively and she was annoyed with herself to find that it thrilled her. She must be going quite mad. She wanted to belong to James, to be his possession, his mistress, anything.

'I'm feeling fine. You know that anyway. They said I would be back to normal in a week and it's been nearly three weeks already. I can do anything now, apparently.'

'I'm glad about that,' he murmured wryly and she flushed deeply, looking away from the dark, mocking eyes, not even pretending to misunderstand.

'Tell me about your aunt.' She had to make some sort of ordinary conversation because he was deliberately making the air around them sing with sensuality. With work left behind he was concentrating his whole magnetism on her, and even his looks made her tremble, his dark power swirling around her.

'Hester? She's a dear. My mother's family were quite wealthy. When she married my father they never recovered from the shock. He was as far beneath her as the earth is to the moon. He came to do some work at my grandfather's house and they met. After that she saw him secretly and married him secretly too. He just moved her away from all of them and for a long time they didn't even know I existed.'

'How did they find out?' When he spoke of his mother that same old bitterness came into his voice and she wished she had never even mentioned it.

'When my mother died, I went to a lot of trouble to find them. I was savagely bitter. I blamed them for lots of things, mainly for not rescuing her. By then there was only one uncle and Aunt Hester. She told me the whole story. I've been close to her ever since. She looks the way Mother would have done if she'd lived. Hester has a corner of my heart.'

'I hope I won't be intruding. I mean...if you usually spend Christmas with her.'

'I used to, until I saw you. After that I spent the week after Christmas with her. The excuse to come to Brightways was gone after the festive season so I then gave my attention to Hester for a few days. You're not intruding, Gemma. She's expecting you.'

There was something so inevitable about the way he spoke of her. He had come to Brightways to merely look at her. Probably if he hadn't he would never have even thought of taking over her father's firm. How different things would have been now. She would have been just as she had always been, shy and uneasy, and Brightways would have fallen into the hands of strangers. It merely added to the feeling of destiny.

'What have you told your aunt?' She looked across at him with anxious eyes and his lips quirked.

'I've told her that with any luck you'll marry me,' he confessed, looking straight ahead. 'I didn't have to promise not to take you to bed at the villa. She's too old-fashioned to even give the matter a thought.'

'So am I!' Gemma looked out of the window, her cheeks red, and his hand covered hers as it trembled on her lap.

'For what it's worth, so am I,' he assured her softly. 'I don't want to seduce you. I want to marry you. In any case, you're still quite weak from the operation.'

'I'm not!' She swung her fair head round and glared at him. 'I'm perfectly fit.' It was only then that she saw the laughter dancing in his eyes.

'All right. So you want me to seduce you. I'll think about it, but don't hold out too many hopes.' He began to laugh softly when she looked at him ferociously and he took her hand again, raising it to his lips with a tender gesture he had never shown before.

'Relax,' he murmured quietly. 'I'm teasing.'

When she leaned back and tried to obey, her heart hammering like mad, he ran his lean fingers over her hand, feeling the texture of her skin, and his voice was warm and low when he spoke again.

'I really don't know what's happening to me,' he confessed wryly. 'I like you, Gemma Lyle. If I didn't want you so damned much I think I would have you for my best friend.'

He couldn't have said anything to please her more and she didn't try to move her hand from his. He had given her self-esteem, a purpose in life and an excitement inside she had never felt before. She loved him and it was no use trying to fool herself. James had become the very centre of her life and the thought of having him out of her life seemed too bleak to imagine.

The wonderful warmth hit them as they landed and Gemma turned her face up to the sun like a cat. Her whole being relaxed and the little pangs of misgiving that had held her fast for the journey fled. Aunt Hester had arranged for her car to be left ready for James and they were soon on their way to the villa. The car was open-topped and the soft wind blew Gemma's hair away from her face. She felt carefree, happy and completely at one with James, even though he didn't know it.

After a while he drove away from the road and down to a secluded inlet where great rocks towered from a deep blue sea. It was beautiful, breathtakingly so, and Gemma sat spellbound as he stopped the car and sat quietly, letting her enjoy the scene.

'Can you see the sea from your aunt's villa?' She turned to him eagerly and he was watching her entranced face. He simply nodded and went on looking at her, not speaking until her questioning looks forced him to say what was on his mind.

'I want you to do something for me, Gemma. I'm dropping it on you suddenly, I know. I'm also expecting you to refuse.'

'What is it?' At this moment she felt so close to him that she was surprised by his hesitation.

'Hester and I are the only two left of the family. We have no one but each other. I care for her. Her health isn't too good; that's why she lives here. She cares for me, too, and she's not at all stupid. She can read the papers and she does. She wants me to settle down. While we're here I want... I would like...' He hesitated and made a wry face. 'I may as well come right out with it,' he muttered in self-disgust. 'I want to make her happy. Wear my ring while you're here, Gemma. Let her imagine we're already engaged to be married.'

For a minute she just looked at him, surprised by his hesitation and his unexpected diffidence. It wasn't like James to almost beg.

'It—it would be cheating, wouldn't it? If you care about her, how can you let her believe something that's not true?' Not knowing what else to say, she fell back on argument and his face darkened, his eyes flashing with the old anger.

'As far as I know this may be her last Christmas. Who can tell what's around the corner for any of us? I intend to marry you anyway. This is merely jumping the gun a little. If you don't feel ready to grant a small favour, look at it this way. I gave you until Christmas to learn the business. I've been strictly fair. You've been in hospital and I'm prepared to extend the time allowance. I'll give you until spring. All I want in return is a little harmless play-acting. I want a fiancée to parade before Hester.'

'James! You're talking as if I've already agreed to marry you,' Gemma protested. 'You said an assessment at Christmas and I didn't even know what you meant. It was a deal, not a foregone conclusion.'

'That's something we can discuss when we get back to England,' he insisted harshly. 'All I want is one small favour. How about it, Gemma? Are you too scared?'

'I'm not scared! I just don't like lying, for any reason, and you—you worry me.'

'Because you don't trust me,' he said flatly.

'Oh, stop it.' She put her hands to her face and looked at him wildly. 'I don't know what to do. As usual you've got me all muddled. If I refuse and anything happens to your aunt I'll feel wicked. If she turns out to be as fit as a fiddle I'll already be enmeshed in lies. No wonder people are scared of you, James Sanderson.'

'Are *you*?' He looked at her evenly and she met the dark gaze squarely.

'No, I'm not. I never have been.' It was true. Deep down she had only been scared of her own feelings and that was still there.

'You said you hated me, Gemma,' he persisted. 'Do you?'

She would have liked to say yes. She would have liked to snap it out and look him defiantly in the eye; but she couldn't find the strength. She didn't hate him; he affected her deeply. He made her tremble, filled her with yearnings she didn't even quite understand. And sometimes she had a ridiculous urge to protect him—as if he needed it.

'No. I don't hate you. How could I? You've been good to me.'

'Have I? I'm sure I never intended to be.' His dark eyes were smiling and she saw the tension in him relax. 'Well?' he challenged. 'Are you going to lie for me?'

'Do I have a lot of choice?' She sighed and held out her hand. 'Get it over with quickly before my conscience gets the better of me. And I warn you, if she's fighting fit I'll make you sorry about this.'

'Threats? We are coming on. Where's the ice-cold girl, the moon-maiden?'

'I worked her out of my system.' Her eyes met his and he smiled, making her heart leap.

'Perhaps it's because you're free, Gemma. For the first time in your life you can say exactly how you feel, with no guilt.'

'I can walk out of Brightways and manage without you,' she pointed out tartly, enjoying this new-found equality. 'I can even get a better job now that I'm a personal assistant.'

'Please don't,' he mocked. 'I'm sure I'd never find a damned thing again without you there.'

Suddenly they were smiling at each other and then he brought out the ring, a large dark sapphire surrounded by diamonds, and Gemma watched almost mesmerised as he slipped it on to her finger. It felt real—as if they were really engaged, as if he had pulled up in this beautiful, romantic spot and proposed to her.

It was a struggle to keep the tears back. One moment she had been almost laughing and now the ring had brought her to the edge of weeping. It was all to comfort an old lady. Gemma didn't know if she was a wicked woman or a pawn in some dark game James was playing. No doubt she could keep the ring if she just gave in and married him, but she would never have James; he had told her that categorically right from the first.

'Tears?' He tilted her face and saw the bright glitter in her eyes. 'It's an emotional moment, getting engaged.'

'I'm not engaged. It's just to fool your aunt. It's not real.'

'We can make it real, Gemma. Any time you want we can make it very real.'

'I don't want to, thank you.' She blinked rapidly, trying to clear her eyes, and he slid his arms around her, pulling her to him.

'You'll never get away from me, Gemma. You're under my skin, in my bloodstream. I want you and I'm going to marry you.'

Her protest was trapped by his lips, never uttered, and she was pulled closer to lie in his arms as he gave way to the desire he had held in close check for weeks.

'No, James!' Knowing her own vulnerability, every defence mechanism came into play. She stiffened and tried to pull away, her hand coming to his lips to stop him when he came after her instantly. His tongue curled around her fingers, licking each one in turn, erotic and exciting, and his lips captured the finger that bore his ring, drawing it into his mouth, sucking rhythmically.

Gemma gave a strange little cry, every defence shattering into a thousand pieces, and he scooped her head towards him, taking her mouth by storm, his hand coming to rest on the swell of her breast.

'You like this, Gemma. We already know that. You like me to touch you here. It sets your heart racing.'

His fingers coaxed her, taking the erect nipple and twisting it gently until every part of her seemed to burst into flame, fierce shafts of feeling that darted downwards to engulf her.

'I want to undress you, to see you again,' he whispered against her ear. 'I want your skin against mine.'

'You promised...' She was sobbing her desire and her protest into his mouth, her breath mingling with his, and he tightened her to him, his breathing uneven.

'I said I didn't approve. I can't promise not to take you, Gemma. You've been on my mind for more than two years and you'll be mine, *soon!*'

His lips covered hers fiercely and she just gave up, surrendering to the desire that raged between them, his fingers urgently slipping open the buttons of her dress and moving inside to close over her breast. It was too sudden, too savage, and she made a little whimper of sound that stopped him instantly.

'I'm hurting you? I don't mean to. Forgive me.'

She had known for a long time that any sign of gentleness from him would be her downfall and now he was gentle, moulding her breast with soothing persuasion, his thumb circling the tight, hard nub. She lifted her head, seeking his lips frantically, and he claimed her mouth, his tongue invading the sweetness with rough, pulsating movements that were suggestive and overwhelming.

Gemma moved against him, sensuality she had not even known she possessed driving her on, and his hand moved beneath her dress to lie flat and warm, heavy against her stomach as if he knew the exact source of her exciting pain. She wanted more, much more, her hips trying to arch against him with age-old instinct, inviting him on, but James drew back.

'No, Gemma,' he whispered thickly. 'I can't take you here. When I make love to you you're going to be my wife.'

Suddenly she was crying, shivering, trembling, her reaction a mixture of frustration and shame. She had wanted him and had made no attempt to move away; in fact she had thrown herself into his arms almost at once. He folded her against him, holding her as she cried, stroking her hair until the gasping sobs subsided.

'I know. I'm leaving you hurting again. Marry me, Gemma. For God's sake give in. You know perfectly well that what's between us is inevitable.' He tilted her face and wiped her eyes, kissing away the last tears. 'If you left, I'd search for you. You know that, don't you? You're the wife I want.'

'Along with your mistress at any given time,' she choked, avoiding his gaze, her own shame defeating her.

'Jealous?' He made her look at him, a light glowing at the back of his dark eyes.

'What do I have to be jealous about?' she managed bitterly. 'To be jealous I would have to love you. I don't!'

His face froze into coldness immediately and he let her go, leaning forward to start the car.

'That makes us even, then,' he said curtly, no sign of gentleness left. 'You're wearing my ring as a favour. I'm extending your time as another favour.'

'And what happens when I run out of time and *still* refuse to marry you?' She was hurting inside, feeling the shaken despair that his coldness brought nowadays. 'It seems to me that I've kept my side of the bargain. I've learned the business and I've learned it fast. By spring I'll be indispensable.'

'Nobody is that,' he assured her coldly. 'If I looked around there would be sure to be another suitable bride, some well-bred and beautiful girl.'

'Then what's all this about?' Gemma felt an almost frightening burst of shock at his words. She had wanted to escape but now she was looking at a cold, hard man who could manage quite well without anyone.

'I want you,' he said flatly, his eyes on the curving road. 'I saw you. I decided and I planned. It's how I am.'

'A take-over bid. An addition to your portfolio,' Gemma muttered angrily, her hand wiping frantically at her still-wet face.

His lips twisted derisively, the dark eyes slanting a look at her that at one time would have scared her.

'Perhaps. But then, I could have taken you not more than a few minutes ago.'

It effectively silenced her and she spent several anxious minutes looking in her mirror, trying to erase any signs of tears. She was a happily engaged woman, her fiancé at her side. She hoped Aunt Hester was not too astute. At the moment she felt incapable of fooling a child.

Gemma knew there were about a hundred and fifty islets and inlets to Bermuda and Aunt Hester owned a villa that nestled in greenery by a silvery beach. She could see the white roof-tops and pink walls of many villas as they approached from a higher road and James pointed out the one that belonged to his only relative. Secluded but not isolated, its green lawns ran down to a sandy beach.

He seemed reluctant to speak to her. The small interlude between them had thrown them back almost to a state of hostility. All Gemma's hard-won courage seemed to have drained away as he became once again a dangerous, silent and dark opponent. She was dreading the arrival. Certainly she was about to appear as a very odd fiancée.

On the quiet road to the villa James stopped the car and turned to look at her steadily. She instantly looked away. If he was going to start again, then she would probably scream and arrive to face his aunt in the middle of a fit of hysterics.

'Perhaps a truce is in order?' His voice was quiet but there was authority there that she refused to acknowledge. She still kept her face firmly turned away.

'I didn't realise there was a battle.'

'There'll be a battle until you're in my arms all night,' he said tersely. 'However, since that's not at all possible we'll have to come to some civilised arrangement. I will not shout at you if you can manage to look less like a captive and more like a fiancée.'

The imperious attitude gained her instant attention and she swung round with blazing eyes.

'*Shout* at me? Just try it and I'll be on the first plane out of here. And let me point out, Mr Sanderson, that I can manage very well without you.' Her annoyance brought a reluctant smile to the hard lips but he wasn't giving much ground.

'In a few minutes you'll be meeting my aunt. No threats, no arguments. *Please* behave yourself.'

'I was brought up with very good manners,' Gemma said huffily, refusing to smile at all. 'I've promised to act this thing out while we're here. I'll keep my word—but only in public.'

'Agreed.' He looked at her quizzically. 'How do I explain your present unhappy condition?'

'You can say I'm not a good traveller, and then, of course, there's my operation.'

'Of course,' he murmured mockingly. 'Subterfuge comes quite easily to you. I should have realised, after the Grainger episode. Let's go on, then. You look as if you needed a little rest.'

'Well, that should break the ice nicely,' Gemma replied in a tart voice. 'Here's my weak-kneed fiancée, Aunt Hester. I would have brought my very powerful mistress, but she had a few walls to push over.'

'I'm really beginning to think you *are* jealous.' His lips quirked and when Gemma glared at him she could see laughter dancing at the back of his dark eyes. Well, it was better than his stormy silence. Maybe his aunt would be fooled?

'Let's get on,' she suggested briskly. 'I'll just practise my smile, so don't bother to speak again.'

This time he grinned openly, but the car rolled forwards and, once again, Gemma turned her head away and looked at the delightful scenery. She really would have to watch her remarks about Roma Prescott, or James's suspicions would turn into certain knowledge. She was finding that jealousy was not too easy to hide.

His aunt was a shock to her. She had become used to thinking of his poor background, of thinking of his mother as a sort of drudge, a woman who was probably badly used, badly dressed, frail and tired.

Aunt Hester looked slightly frail but there any connection with the family of Gemma's imagination stopped. Hester Somers was tall and blue-eyed, her face definitely aristocratic, her slender, blue-veined hands covered with glittering rings.

There was nothing browbeaten about her at all. She was, in her own way, as commanding a figure as James, and she obviously adored him. He was hugged and kissed, to his clear amusement and pleasure, and then the blue eyes turned on Gemma.

'So this is Gemma?' she said with a rather impish grin. 'This is the girl who's going to save you from the black pit. My dear, I'm just delighted. It's time this rogue was settled and brought to heel.'

'I'm brought to heel already,' James pointed out, lifting Gemma's hand to show the ring on her finger. His arm came tightly and threateningly around her and his aunt kissed her cheeks warmly.

'So you agreed?' she said softly. 'I so hoped you would, but then, James usually gets what he wants, as

I expect you know. I did wonder if it would be so easy with someone he really cared about. I don't suppose he ordered you to become engaged?' she added with an amused look.

'No. It—it was a m-mutual agreement.'

'She stammers when she's embarrassed, don't you, darling?' James put in quickly when his aunt looked surprised. 'She's also had a very bad flight. Let's show her to her room.'

It was the best thing he could have said. Gemma had taken an instant liking to the elderly lady and guilt was coming over her in waves like the sea, making her cheeks glow with shame.

'Of course, dear. Oh, but do let her meet Sheena first.' She smiled at a woman who had just come in. 'Gemma, this is my nurse, Miss Radcliffe, but I don't suppose she'll mind at all if you call her Sheena. She's been here with me for the past five years.'

Gemma turned with a smile that almost died on her face. Miss Radcliffe looked more like a fashion model than a nurse. She was about thirty, tall and slim, her hair dark red, her face most definitely beautiful, and Gemma remembered that James had come here each year, probably more than once, if the welcoming looks on the woman's face were to be believed.

He knew her. It was impossible to stop the flare of dismay. She also remembered thinking that every woman in the Sanderson-Lyle building was in love with James. He had always had a vibrant attraction for women, and the look in Sheena Radcliffe's eyes assured Gemma that here was another one. How would she cope here with them both right under her nose? She couldn't bear it if...

Sheena smiled seductively at James and stood very carefully posed in the doorway.

'Oh, James! How lovely to see you again!' She came hurrying across to him and Gemma turned away. If he was going to kiss her hello, then she just didn't want to see it. He did no such thing but he gave her one of those smiles that he reserved for beautiful ladies.

'Sheena. You're more beautiful than ever.'

Gemma waited for her to say something trite and she did.

'It's the excitement of seeing you, James.'

Hester intervened very quickly, her fine forehead slightly creased in what was almost a frown.

'And this is the girl he's going to marry, Sheena,' she pointed out firmly. 'They're actually engaged. I can't tell you how happy it makes me. Isn't she lovely to look at?'

'And delightful to know,' James put in smoothly, his arm tightening again around Gemma's slim waist. 'You can help me to keep an eye on her, Sheena. She's just had an appendix operation.'

'I'm quite recovered!' Gemma said hastily. She didn't much fancy being ordered to bed by Sheena Radcliffe while James sunned himself on the beach and Aunt Hester had an afternoon nap. She knew where the nurse would be then.

Her room faced the sea. Hester took her along to it while James collected the bags from the car. As they stepped to the window they could see him; Sheena Radcliffe had gone out with him and they were laughing together, a thing that James rarely did with Gemma.

'I had to leave my car at the airport for James,' Hester said quickly, turning her away from the window. 'Visitors aren't allowed to hire cars, you know, not here—although James could easily...'

Gemma knew that Hester was quite deliberately keeping her mind off the fact that Sheena was standing very close to James.

'It's a lovely room,' she said softly. 'Thank you for having me here.'

'My dear, I'm really so happy. James means a lot to me. I never had children of my own. I know he loves you. I can see it written in his eyes. I want you to come here as often as you can.' She patted Gemma's arm and turned to the door. 'I'll let James bring your things. When he's not hanging about, you and I must have a little talk.'

It had a worrying sound and Gemma regretted this deceit, whatever James's motives had been. His aunt was a lovely woman and not too strong either, by the look of her; at least that bit had been true. Still, she thought fairly, she had never known James to lie, not until now.

He came in with the bags then, and she heard him coming and used the beautiful scene from her window as an excuse to keep her face turned away from him. She felt quite shaken by her own burst of jealousy and James always saw far too much. There was a lot for him to see if he was looking for clues. Every time she saw him now it was like seeing him for the first time, and she knew that if she had been seeing him for the first time she would have fallen in love at once, would have walked like a sleep-walker towards him and into his arms if he had ordered it. She had completely changed.

'Is anything wrong, Gemma?' he asked quietly, standing by the door as he put her suitcase down. 'You look—strained. You've lost that little bit of weight again too. Maybe I should tie you down in case of strong winds.'

She said nothing at all; in fact she was still too upset to turn, but he came to her and turned her anyway, looking at her intently.

'What do you think of Hester?'

'I liked her on sight. She's unexpected.'

'Considering my background?' he asked drily. 'She's from my mother's side of the family.'

'Stop putting words into my mouth,' Gemma protested hotly. 'You've got a fixation about your background. No wonder you're so hard; it's not natural to keep living in the past.'

'The only fixation I have is about you,' he murmured, pulling her towards him, 'and that's very natural.'

His lips touched hers gently and then more deeply as he gathered her completely into his arms, and it was no contest because she couldn't resist James. Her arms wound around his neck and her lips parted as he opened his mouth over hers.

When he lifted his head she was trembling all over and he looked down at her intently.

'Gemma——' he began.

'Shall I unpack for you, James?' Sheena Radcliffe was already in the doorway as she spoke, and Gemma pulled away fretfully. How many more mistresses were going to break in upon them? Her hot face was more rage than embarrassment.

'No, thank you, Sheena,' James said calmly. 'I'll unpack for myself when I've got Gemma settled. She needs a rest. I'll see you on the veranda in a minute. You can bring me up to date on things.'

Miss Radcliffe's lips curved in triumph as she left. Here was another woman who wasn't at all put off by the idea of a forthcoming marriage—not if she could have James.

'How do you imagine we're going to keep this subterfuge with your friend behind every door?' Gemma snapped in a low voice. 'Miss Radcliffe is going to be one step behind you all the time. It's going to be like old-time dancing!'

'I seem to remember saying that *you* were my friend,' he murmured, his eyes on her angry face. "Surely you don't expect me to ignore Sheena? I've known her for ages; I was the one who found her for Aunt Hester.'

'I can well believe it! As to being your friend, I'm nothing of the sort and you know it. I'm in this situation because we have a deal, that's all.'

'Is it?' He looked down at her threateningly. 'And why do you behave so sweetly in my arms?'

'Sheer feminine instinct,' she snapped, wild with jealous rage and hurting inside. 'After all, it's not hard, you being such an experienced man. I imagine any experienced man could do that to me.'

He grabbed her by the shoulders, a rage on his face that quite outclassed her own small fury, and for a moment she really saw the devil in him. At the sight of her suddenly white face, he let her go and turned to the door.

'I'll see you later,' he said darkly, adding derisively, 'Thank you for keeping your voice low. Any time you want to rage at me, we'll walk along the beach.'

He went, and Gemma stood by the window fighting tears. Clearly he had not gone to unpack because she saw him almost immediately step down to the beach, his hand lifted to help Sheena Radcliffe. They walked along by the sea and after a moment Sheena clung to his arm. Gemma could hear them laughing.

What was the use? What did she hope for after all? He certainly didn't love her and never would. This was what she could expect every day of her life if she gave in to the primitive urge to marry him and cling. She slipped off her dress and went to lie on the bed, and after a few minutes she fell asleep, more exhausted by her own emotions than by the long journey.

CHAPTER EIGHT

DINNER was difficult because Sheena joined them. Of course there was nothing unusual about that. Miss Radcliffe was a sort of nurse-companion as far as Gemma could make out, and it would have been very odd if she hadn't been treated like one of the family. Gemma asked herself seriously if she would have liked the woman if there had been no involvement with James, and she had to admit that she would not. There was something about her that reminded Gemma of Roma Prescott. Maybe he liked women like that—glossy and glamorous and filled with hard, vibrant energy?

Gemma tried her best to make conversation, but it was hard going, especially as she could see Sheena constantly smiling at James. He talked to Sheena too—almost exclusively—while Hester was left to entertain Gemma.

'James was telling me about your beautiful house—Brightways, isn't it?'

'Yes. It's beautiful,' Gemma agreed. 'It's not mine, though, not now. James bought it when my father died.'

'I don't suppose it matters really, does it?' Hester asked gently. 'I expect you'll live there when you're married?'

It left Gemma in a fix, but before she could either lie or tell the truth James intervened.

'Yes. We'll live there. That's the only reason I bought the house. I think Gemma would simply fade away without Brightways. Her life revolves around it.'

There was an underlying harshness to his voice that his aunt seemed to miss, but Gemma didn't miss it and neither, apparently, did Sheena. She looked from one to the other with a great deal of calculating interest.

'I shall come to England for the wedding, climate or not,' Hester said determinedly. 'When is it?'

'Gemma hasn't fixed the date yet,' James said blandly. 'Don't worry, though, we'll let you know in good time.'

'Maybe you should rush her,' Hester remarked with a mischievous smile. '"Faint heart never won fair lady." She might refuse if you leave it too long.'

'She won't refuse,' James murmured, his dark eyes on Gemma's flushed face. 'I've got her securely trapped, haven't I, angel?'

'Well, that's one way of putting it,' Gemma replied, gazing at her ring that sparkled in the lights. 'Besides, I have to think of the upset it would cause if I left you. The great James Sanderson—jilted. I don't think I could face the repercussions.'

'I'm glad you said that.' James smiled and Gemma supposed that to the others it was a loving smile. She, though, could see the threat behind it. When she finally walked out on James it was not going to be easy, she knew that.

Later they sat on the veranda, James keeping up conversation with his aunt, and this time Sheena Radcliffe seemed to be unsure. She hovered around with a smile on her face that said she was waiting for an invitation.

'Do join us, Sheena,' Hester said in her usual gracious manner, and that was all it took. She came forward with a fervent smile at James, and managed to sit herself close to him. It did not please his aunt. Having got James to the stage of engagement, she was clearly determined that marriage should follow, and from then on she seemed to be only half listening to Gemma, her eyes straying frequently to Sheena's laughing face.

Gemma felt as if she were sitting on top of a powder-keg, and stood to go into the villa, but James caught her wrist as she passed, looking up at her.

'Walk on the beach?' he suggested with enough gentleness to have his aunt relaxing again.

'If you like.'

She didn't want to. She didn't want to be alone with James at all, but there was nothing she could do. If he was playing this by ear he had certainly pleased his aunt, and the tension began to ease a little, except inside Gemma. He kept his hold on her wrist as if she would bolt and then his hand closed warmly round hers, his fingers lacing with her own. She was aware of the others watching as they walked off and was not really surprised to hear Hester's voice.

'They're so close. You can see it. I never thought it would happen to James. I can't tell you how pleased I am.' There was a very satisfied sound to her voice. Gemma didn't hear Sheena's reply but she could only imagine it was some trite, expected thing.

Then they were away from the sound of the voices and she pulled her hand free, more because she badly wanted to keep it in his warm fingers than anything else. He walked quietly beside her, beginning after a second to pick up large pebbles and throw them to skim on the calm sea. They leapt across the surface of the dark water with a life of their own.

'Bet you can't do this,' he murmured.

'You're right. I used to try until my arm felt as if it would drop off.'

She found herself smiling and stopped walking to watch the white pebbles leaping and bouncing across the surface of the sea.

'Care to try it now?' James handed her a flat, smooth pebble.

'No! No, thank you.' She almost snatched her hand away.

'We have to pass the time until we can decently go back. Hester is expecting a nice, romantic interlude. Of course, if you can think of anything else to fill in the time...'

She didn't seem to have much choice and she was no better at this sport than she had been years ago. Her stones sank like stones and she looked at James with angry frustration, childishly annoyed at his easy skill in everything.

'Wrong arm action,' he informed her smoothly, handing her another missile. 'No ease of movement. You're trying too hard. The thing to do is get the right action and then enjoy it.'

'It's stupid!'

'Then why are you so annoyed? Trying to be like someone else leads to great stress.'

She could hear laughter in his voice and she snapped at him immediately. 'I'm not trying to be like anyone. Who would I want to imitate?'

'Me,' he said softly, coming and taking her arm, turning her to the sea. 'It's useless, you know. You're not made of the same hard material. You're trying to get the better of me to prove you don't need me. You do need me and I prefer you to be yourself, however irritating.' He lifted her arm. 'Let's get back to the present. Back like this, turn the wrist and release smoothly.'

It skimmed across the water, dancing and bouncing into the dusk, and Gemma felt a burst of feeling as she realised how James was holding her. He was very close, too close, his eyes on her face as she turned her head. She saw her mistake then. He had coaxed all anger out of her, all tension and his slow smile acknowledged his own victory.

'You're a late achiever, perhaps? We can't spend the rest of our lives throwing pebbles. When do you belong to me, Gemma?'

'I never will.' She tried to move but his other arm came round her waist, his hand leaving her arm to tilt her face back as he pulled her close, her shoulders against his chest.

He never bothered to answer; he just kissed her slowly and deeply, holding her against him on the quiet beach with darkness gathering around them, turning her into his arms when she just gave in and clung to his lips as if she needed him to keep her alive.

'How long do you think you can hold out against me?' he murmured softly as he lifted his head and looked down at her, and the deep sound of his voice, taunting and sure, brought her back out of the trance. She spun free and raced towards the villa, her heart pounding frantically. James could make her do anything. He had her to the stage where she would almost beg at his feet.

She came to her senses and stopped at the veranda. She could hardly go charging inside like this. Hester would need no telling that something had happened. In her own way she was almost as astute as James.

Luckily they had gone inside now and it was almost dark anyway. She sat on the steps, frustrated and trapped, trying to still her heartbeats and the excitement that only James could arouse. She had no alternative but to wait for him.

He came strolling out of the darkness and she looked up at him, her voice trembling when she spoke.

'Why are you doing this? You have no right to...'

'Right?' he grated savagely. 'It seems to me that I merely have responsibilities. I'll shoulder those responsibilities more easily when you're mine. As to kissing you, I like it. You're kissable and a lot more besides.'

He took her arm, pulling her to her feet. 'Let's get inside and bring an end to this day,' he added irascibly. 'I'm tired.'

They ate Christmas lunch and then sat on the beach. It would have been enjoyable but the fact that Sheena Radcliffe was also there forced Gemma's problems more deeply into her mind. There would always be someone, some woman for James. With his aunt there he was careful but Gemma didn't miss the looks that Sheena threw his way, nor did she miss the way his eyes answered. She wished she had stayed in England and not been forced to witness all this. Any ease with James was now gone and most of the tension was coming from herself, and she had no doubts about why. Jealousy.

He had wanted Sheena Radcliffe out here to amuse him when he spent time with his aunt. He had even chosen the nurse himself. He couldn't even spend a small time away from some woman or other and, as she watched him stretched out on the beach, Gemma could understand why. His aura of sensuality was almost tangible.

She watched him laughing and talking, her heart quite heavy. Sheena was wearing a black bikini but Gemma had been more circumspect. She didn't want to see James's cynical eyes on her at all. She had covered her bikini with an ankle-length beach-wrap and James looked across at her with barely concealed amusement, well able to follow her reasoning.

'That's nice,' Hester said. 'That blue colour suits you. It's the same as your eyes.'

'They're purple,' James remarked, merely interrupting his conversation with the nurse and never even looking round now. 'Purple with gold flecks.'

It gave the impression that he was accustomed to looking deeply into her eyes, and Gemma blushed as Sheena shot her a look of annoyance. It had sounded possessive and his aunt went back to her knitting with a small smile of satisfaction on her face. No doubt she thought them an odd couple, but she assumed that things were all right, all the same. It was a good job that James was not leaving the play-acting to her, Gemma thought. She hardly dared to look at him. It was beginning to hurt too much.

She was lying with her eyes closed when James made an alarming announcement.

'I'm taking Gemma sailing for a few hours. Will you feel neglected?'

Gemma opened her eyes quickly to see him standing looking down at his aunt, who smiled serenely.

'How can I be neglected, James, when Sheena is here? Run along, I know Gemma will enjoy it.'

If Gemma hadn't been all hot and cold at the idea of being alone with James, she would have laughed at the subtlety. Hester was getting her order in first. Miss Radcliffe was not to accompany them on any trip.

'Right. That leaves me with a clear conscience.' He reached down to Gemma, holding his hand out. 'Come along, angel.'

'I—I'll change into trousers and shirt...'

'You're expecting a force-ten gale?' His perfect mouth curved. 'You'll do fine as you are. I've got a nice little cruiser here. We're not rowing anywhere.'

He didn't even give her the chance to go into the villa. He took her hand firmly and led her off towards the small boat-house that stood at the edge of the water while Sheena lay looking after them intently.

'Don't struggle,' James warned. 'Just come along nicely. We're being watched.'

'I did notice! Surely you feel mean, leaving Sheena?'

'Not really. I want you to myself. It's the only reason I brought you out here. Sheena is the persistent type but don't let it worry you.'

'Why should it?' Gemma snapped in a low voice. 'She's nothing to me, after all. Neither are you.'

'There, you said that very nicely as if you'd learnt it off by heart. So, as we're nothing to each other, relax. I've got something to show you.'

The boat was a cabin-cruiser of medium size, gleaming and white. It was the first time in her life that Gemma had been on a boat and she felt a wave of excitement that quite chased away her gloom. With a skill he showed in everything else, James soon had them under way and skimming across the shimmering water.

'Where are we going?' she shouted over the noise of the engines and James answered without turning his head, his eyes on the outline of a small island, wooded and green, that was rapidly growing in size as they came closer.

'Right there.' He nodded ahead, his lean brown hands on the wheel. 'It's quiet and peaceful, just the place to relax. We can swim in perfect safety. It's a much more serene place than the spot where Hester had her villa built.'

James cut the engine and they coasted in close to the shore as Gemma stood and surveyed the golden beach, the swaying trees that came almost to the water's edge in places.

'It looks private. I don't like trespassing.'

Her anxiety brought a rather cynical smile to his lips.

'Of course you imagine that I do? It's astonishing how we always seem to get back to my beginnings. Honestly, I haven't stolen apples for years. I'm almost respectable. On a dark night you'd never notice.'

His sarcasm dispelled the wave of excitement Gemma was beginning to feel at being with him, and she turned her head away, refusing to answer or be goaded into any argument. Now that they were alone there was a distinctly dangerous air about him and she wished she had pleaded tiredness and refused to come. Not that any pleading would have impressed James. He wanted something and he got it.

'This place is mine,' he assured her curtly when she stood there in silence. 'I bought it a long time ago but as yet I haven't got around to building any sort of house here. I simply stay with Hester when I come over. There's more company.'

Like Sheena! Gemma bit into her soft lip and said nothing, but the thought of his being here with Sheena took all the enjoyment out of the afternoon.

She sat on deck and made no move to swim—not even when James went below and returned in brief black trunks and dived over the side of the boat into the clear blue sea. The sun was hot and she wanted desperately to take off her beach-wrap and join him in the cool water. She would have done except for the taunting look in his eyes.

For a while she watched him swimming strongly close to the boat, circling it like a shark, something very suggestive in his actions—as if he was keeping her here away from everyone else. He dived and she felt a quick flush of relief that the dark eyes were no longer on her, and when he surfaced he was well away from the boat, heading for the beach with long, powerful strokes. He had simply gone off and left her.

Annoyance drove her to her feet. She knew perfectly well that she had been sulking on deck, refusing to even call out to him, but his desertion was a reprimand she refused to accept. She didn't need him anyway!

She pulled off her wrap and stood poised for a second in the skimpy dark blue bikini she had been at such pains to conceal, and then she dived cleanly into the water, rising at once to swim around the whole boat, repeatedly diving to look into the clear depths, determined to enjoy herself and, yes, determined to be as good as James.

She was not as good as James, though. She had never been a powerful swimmer and a spell in hospital hadn't helped at all. She looked towards the boat and it seemed a long way off. How had she managed to get so far away? She tried to relax but all she did was sink and she came back to the surface struggling frantically.

Inside there was a terrible fright growing. She could never swim back to the boat; nor could she make it to the beach.

'Oh, James!' Was that little whimper of sound her own voice? Was this how it would happen, so carelessly, and would James care, really care? She suddenly knew that without James she would find no joy in anything for the rest of her life anyway.

When strong arms grasped her she was on the point of exhaustion, but even so she struggled until she turned her head and saw him. His face was furious and after one look at her he turned her on to her back and began to tow her strongly towards the beach. She made no attempt to help because she couldn't. In those few minutes she had seemed to live a lifetime and also to die a little. And she had faced her own heart squarely.

'What the hell were you doing?'

He lifted her as soon as their feet touched the sandy bottom and carried her on to the beach, before lying her down and kneeling to look into her pale face.

'I thought...I thought I was strong enough to—to...' Tears flooded her eyes and slowly trickled down her face, but still he watched her with every sign of temper, a man she knew only too well could be icy with rage.

'Well?' He wasn't helping now and he evidently expected some explanation of her odd conduct. 'When I left you, you were sitting serenely on the deck. The next time I looked the deck was empty and you were swimming like a lunatic, diving and coming up. Damn you, Gemma! I didn't even know you could swim. I thought you'd fallen over the side and might drown at any time.'

'I—I didn't know it would be so hard... It's ages since I swam. You seemed to be occupied, anyway.'

The anger left his face to be replaced by much more subtle emotions. 'I was on the beach, down there.' He pointed but she was too weary to lift her head and look. 'I was just wondering where I would build.'

'You left me.' It was a plaintive little cry and she turned her head away, instantly ashamed.

'I didn't leave you,' he corrected quietly. 'I thought you didn't want to join me and I got too frustrated just looking at you. I went ashore for a minute.' He grimaced wryly. 'I thought I had everything under control. I thought you were safely seated and well covered up.'

'You could have *told* me!' Now that she was safe she was angry, sitting up to glare at him. He had no idea how she felt about him. He would never love her. There was just desire. 'I might have wanted to come with you and look too.'

He pushed her gently back. 'I didn't think you wanted to know,' he said quietly. 'Sometimes I just can't go on looking at you, Gemma. I have to take off and work out my frustration on something else.' He gave a wary little laugh. 'If the materials had been there I might have started building the damned house right then.' He stood and brushed the sand from his legs. 'Come on. I'll get you back.'

Gemma didn't want to move. Suddenly she was sleepy, heavy lids drooping over her eyes, her lashes brushing her cheeks where now a little colour had returned. The sun was already drying her skin and the bikini and she wanted to turn on her side and curl up.

She put her head on her arm and gave in to the feeling. 'Just give me a minute.'

'You can't sleep here. You'll be burned.'

'Just a minute—please.'

'How can I refuse such a weary pleading? A minute, then, until I fetch the dinghy,' he agreed. 'You'll not even be able to get on board if I tow you back. Stay here, and this time I mean it. If you've moved when I get back...'

'I couldn't.' Her lips curved into a smile of sheer luxury at the idea of lying on the soft sand and sleeping, and, after an intent look at her, he turned and plunged into the warm sea.

She must have dozed off to sleep instantly because she never heard the noise of the outboard motor as James returned. The first thing she knew he was kneeling beside her, shaking her gently.

'Wake up, Gemma, we're going back to the boat.'

'Have we been here long?' Disorientated, she raised sleepy eyes and looked up into his dark face.

'Hardly any time at all,' he assured her, pulling her to her feet. 'There must be something of the Rip Van Winkle in you; it's merely minutes since I left you and now you can't remember where you are.'

'I can. We're on your little island. I'm tired because I'm stupid. I wore myself out. *Next* time...'

'There'll be no "next time" because after this fiasco I'll remember that you survive best in an evening gown.' With this taut comment he left her to make her way to the dinghy all by herself. Apparently he was so frustrated with her that he couldn't even manage to walk beside her. Well, she didn't need him, either!

The sun was hot, more than she had realised, and walking on deep, soft sand was awkward. There was also a certain amount of lethargy, a legacy of her relief. There was an unreal feeling too. She was in love for the first time in her life. She wanted to wrap her arms round James and tell him but she was not—and never would be—*that* stupid.

Something made her feel strange, though, and she suddenly suffered a wave of dizziness that actually forced her to her knees. The whole landscape of sand and sky seemed to rock and she put her head in her hands, closing her eyes.

'Gemma?'

James came back quickly and she looked up to see him standing over her, his legs strong and brown, his magnificent chest broad and muscular. The world began to spin again and she moaned softly, covering her eyes.

'What's wrong?' He crouched down beside her and she was too taken up with this sudden dizziness to worry about him.

'I don't know. Everything is spinning. It just happened suddenly.'

'Lie back a minute.' He sounded very concerned and she did exactly as she was told, closing her eyes and shielding them from the sun.

'I expect it's the unaccustomed exercise. I'm not really fit at the moment.'

He came down beside her and when she opened her eyes he was looking concerned and angry at the same time.

'You do the most ridiculous things. Did you have to dive in and try to prove you're as good as me?'

The dizziness had somewhat subsided and she sat up, her eyes black with annoyance. Here she was, *suffering* for him, and all he could do was chastise her.

'I didn't try to prove anything. It was irresponsible of you to go off like that,' she snapped. Even mentioning it upset her again and his face softened somewhat.

'So you wanted me to be with you. You care about me.' His voice was quiet, insistent, and Gemma's face flushed with embarrassment.

'I do not! I would have been annoyed if anyone had taken me out and then deserted me. It's not what I'm used to. Your company would have been acceptable. I was prepared to overlook just who you are.'

He stood in one lithe movement, scooping her up into his arms.

'My poor little maniac. Let's get you on board. You need a drink. I think the sun's got to you. I always knew it wouldn't take much to drive you over the top.'

'Just because I don't care about you?' She was trembling almost at once when he touched her and now, being in his arms, her bikini her only covering, she was terribly aware of his skin next to hers.

'You do, Gemma. I'm not blind. I can feel you trembling.'

'It's shock.'

'Little fool.' He didn't look down at her. He just continued walking, wading into the sea and setting her down in the swaying dinghy. 'I'm not so easy to lose and I have no intention at all of losing you.'

On the boat he poured her a cool drink and watched her as she drank it almost greedily.

'You probably swallowed half the bay. Most of the beach is on you at the moment, too. You can get a shower.'

'When I get back to the villa.' She was proud of her firm, haughty voice, not being able to hear the tremor that ran through it.

'You'll get it here. Right through that way.' He nodded to a sliding-door. 'I need a shower, too; hesitate much longer and I'll join you, Miss Lyle.'

It was a superb threat and Gemma obeyed, feeling better as the cool water played over her skin. She slid one slender arm out of the door, reaching for her robe, and James put it into her hand.

'Pass me the bikini. I'll dry it off,' he ordered and she stepped out, securely wrapped in her beach-robe, and reluctantly handed him the flimsy articles. He was already in a robe himself and she combed out her hair, watching him fasten both the costumes outside in the hot sunshine.

'Peculiar flags,' he remarked wryly, coming back to the shower. 'I do hope Hester hasn't got her binoculars out.'

He spared her blushes by stepping into the shower and Gemma walked into the cabin. She didn't feel like going into the sun. Now that it was all over and she was safely back on the boat she felt let down, strangely empty, wanting something she couldn't even put a name to. She lay back on the long padded seat, putting her head back and closing her eyes.

'Sleeping again?' James was standing over her, towelling his dark hair, his robe tightly round him.

'No. I—I was thinking. I feel odd.'

'In pain?'

'Of course not. I didn't injure myself.' She gave a little smile. 'Well, perhaps my dignity.'

'I was thinking about your operation.'

'For goodness' sake! I've told you already that I'm better. Even the doctor agrees. If I hadn't been, do you imagine I could have dived off the boat and swam around like—like...?'

'Like someone in despair? You thought I'd lost interest in you.'

'I imagined you were being your usual angry self. That's different.'

'It would be, if it were true. You care about me, Gemma. Admit it.' He came to sit by her, dangerously close.

'I don't!' she denied frantically, trying to turn away, struggling to get up. It was dangerous here with James; she had been right. He looked even more dangerous now to her agitated mind. His hands held her shoulders, though, and she was left looking up into his eyes.

'Yes, you do, and there's no reason to let it kill you. I'm here.'

He lowered himself against her, his body brushing hers and she shook her head, her eyes mournful.

'Don't, James. Don't do this to me. Why do you keep on . . . ?'

'I want you. You want me too.'

'I don't——' Her shaken denial was cut off by his mouth as he lifted her into his arms and closed her lips with his own.

Instantly tears began, flooding her eyes, rolling to her cheeks, and he raised his head, cupping her face, his fingers stroking against her skin.

'Shh, Gemma. Shh.' He kissed the tears away, kissed her trembling lips, making tiny, tasting bites at her mouth and her cheeks, her neck and her shoulders, until she twisted against him.

'Don't, James!' she pleaded brokenly, but her eyes were pleading for more and he saw it.

'Angel, it's sheer necessity.' He gathered her close and she responded as if it was fate, her gasp purely joy as his lips closed over her own urgently.

He lifted her, carrying her through to the bunk, and she was almost weightless. It would always be like this with James. The fight would always go out of her when

he touched her. If he had touched her two years ago it
would all have happened then.

He placed her on the bunk and came down to her,
and his body felt powerful, his hips moving restlessly
against hers as she wound her arms around his neck
tightly. She felt the hard arousal of his body, even
through the thickness of the robes, and her own body
reacted with shocked delight, moulding itself against him
mindlessly, the taut pressure of his thighs sending shafts
of excitement through her. She arched against him,
pressing herself closer, and he came down heavily on
her, the sweet smell of soap mixing with the more subtle
scent of desire.

'James!' She threw her head back, already abandoned to him, and he kissed the arched length of her
neck, his mouth moving down to search for her hardened
nipple beneath the thick fabric.

It was too much of a barrier between them in her wild
delight and she tossed her head from side to side,
moaning in tiny whispers, her cries changing to heated
gasps when he pulled aside the robe and caressed her
breast with his tongue. Her body was alive with desire
for him, his every action sending waves of aching need
through her, and she clutched at his shoulders, gasping
his name.

'I want you against me,' he said thickly. 'I want
nothing at all between us.' He shrugged out of his robe
and removed hers, his eyes flaring over her. 'Tell me
now if I can't have you,' he whispered huskily, his strong
hand curving around the silken weight of her breast.
'This has got to stop now or go on completely. You know
that.'

'I know!' It was a long, shuddering sigh and his face
darkened, desire colouring his high cheekbones, his knee
parting her legs almost of its own volition.

'I want you now,' he whispered almost savagely.

Passion flared between them like a fire, their lips fusing together, and his hands moved over her with total possession. She was his and he knew it. He looked down at her, his heated gaze lingering on her breasts and then moving over her face.

'At this moment I could devour you. I want to see you carrying my child!'

The way he said it, the harsh intention, shocked Gemma out of delight and she tightened up inside, memory of his original proposal surfacing belatedly. He wanted her for a bride to round off a brilliant career, and a child to inherit his wealth, and he was making sure he got it.

What about her? What about the rest of her life? The child would never be hers really; James would train it in his own image—hard and brilliant. And the women would continue, on and on forever, because he really cared for no one at all, least of all for her.

He was watching her, seeing the light die out of her eyes while his own eyes were almost black with passion.

'Gemma!' he grated thickly and she knew that there would be no turning back if she didn't fight now in the only way she could. If he held her again, made love to her at all, she would surrender. It was fight or die slowly over the long years, because he would never release a possession and that was all she would ever be.

'I can't stop you, James,' she managed. 'You can make me want you. We both know it. Whatever happens, though, afterwards, I'll never marry you. I want you to know that too.'

She would always remember how he looked then, his face paled with shock, his eyes starkly black, and he said nothing at all. He simply sat up and put his robe on, tossing her hers, and then he was out on the deck. A few seconds later he threw her bikini on to the bunk and walked out to start the engine.

Somehow, while she was getting ready, her bikini now bone dry, he had dressed, and though she sat on deck as they went back she didn't try to speak. She knew James too well by now. It was all quite over.

CHAPTER NINE

JAMES finally spoke, though, just before they came in to the landing-stage at the villa.

'Why, Gemma?' His voice sounded raw and she couldn't answer. She avoided his gaze by fastening her wrap more closely around her, wasting time until he was almost explosive.

'Look at me, Gemma, damn you!' he rasped thickly, but she refused, hanging her head.

'I don't want to, James. I don't even want to look at myself. I feel cheap.'

'*What?*' His voice was appalled, ferocious, as she had known it would be, and she looked up, her face composed now.

'I can't help how I feel, James,' she said steadily, forcing herself to meet his wide, angry eyes. 'I feel cheap, whether I should or not.'

He didn't speak again but when they landed he took her arm in a grip of steel and marched her back across the beach, white to the lips with rage, and it was only as they approached his aunt, who was sitting contentedly looking at the sea, that his grip relaxed.

'Why, Gemma, dear. Are you all right?' Hester asked anxiously as she looked round and saw Gemma's face. James cut in before Gemma could speak.

'She's tired. I think it's the sun.'

'Yes. I'll just go for a rest,' Gemma got out fast before Hester could suggest that Sheena came to look at her. In any case, she wanted to get away from James and his taut, angry face. His rage seemed to be hanging in the air, a black cloud of it around him.

When James looked in later she simply kept her eyes closed and feigned sleep. It was cowardly but it was all she could think to do. James was not the sort of person to accept humble apologies and, in any case, it would only put her right back where she had been before—utterly at his mercy.

He walked over to the bed and looked down at her as she lay perfectly still, and he wasn't fooled at all.

'I know you're in there,' he said in a sort of menacing growl. 'Never mind, though, Hester and the servants won't let you die and I'm going out. I'm going out with Sheena.'

That was enough to anger her too, to have her eyes coming wide open. 'I suggest you go, then,' she advised. 'In any case, you shouldn't be in here. What your aunt would think . . .'

'I'm beyond caring what people think!' he muttered with ragged ferocity. 'I only know what *I* think. You want me, you care about me, but you'll die rather than admit it. What is it, Gemma—the princess and the stable boy syndrome? You're afraid I'll disgrace you in public, eat peas off my knife? Don't let it trouble you. I cope very well, even if I make you feel cheap.'

'I didn't mean . . .'

'Spare me, Gemma,' he grated. 'You make yourself quite clear on every occasion. I have no doubt at all about what you think of me.'

He just walked out and Gemma lay there looking at the closed door. It had simply never occurred to her that he would take it like that. She could not have chosen a worse way of getting herself out of a situation. Did he really believe she felt that marrying him would be beneath her? Would she have to confess to loving him to make any sense of this at all? His world was awash with women—one right in this house—and yet he wanted *her*. Perhaps now he would ignore her, and she had no idea how she would feel about that.

To protect herself she had hurt and angered James, and the contempt in his voice had been as burning as his kisses. Sheena Radcliffe would be in his arms, smiling up into his face. What would Hester think now? After all this subterfuge about the engagement he was showing clearly that he didn't care at all. Was she going to be the one who had to explain?

She couldn't stay at Brightways now, not any more. The time had come to stand firmly on her own two feet, to break free of the past and James.

She didn't stay in bed. It seemed dreadful to cringe here when Hester was alone. She waited to hear the car leave and then got dressed and went to find his aunt.

'Why, Gemma! Should you be up?' It was heartening to see genuine concern on Hester's face. 'James seemed to think you would be staying in bed.'

'I'm all right,' Gemma assured her. 'I brought it all on with my own foolishness. I haven't taken any exercise for ages and I jumped into the sea and swam around like a lunatic. I surely asked for it.'

'Well, I'm really surprised that James allowed that,' Hester said sternly. 'I thought he had more than his fair share of common sense.'

'He does, but he wasn't there.' Trying to get James off the hook seemed to have her right on it and she found Hester's bright eyes intent on her, expecting some explanation. 'James left me for a while and I wanted to swim. I bit off more than I could chew.' Gemma looked up and smiled wryly. 'He wasn't too pleased.'

'I can imagine,' Hester laughed. 'Well, that's a relief. It explains his black scowls. I thought for a while...' She looked at Gemma consideringly. 'I suppose I'm always expecting the worst. I never believed that James would marry. I never thought he would be able to tell any woman that he loved her. Strong and successful though he is, there's a wide streak of vulnerability in James. He had a very bad childhood.'

'I know.' Gemma met the clear eyes. 'He told me about his mother—well, not much, but enough for me to realise the unhappiness.'

'She was never a battered wife, Gemma.' Hester's lips tightened. 'That brute kept his violence for James. I sometimes find it hard to forgive Marion for not coming home to the family, if only for the sake of her son; but James understands. She loved her husband—enough to forgive his violence, enough to see James sink into a hard shell of self-protection. I always imagined that if James loved anyone at all it would only be me, because I look like my sister in many ways. When you came with him I was overjoyed, and that's the greatest under-statement of the year.'

Gemma's eyes were on her own tightly clenched fingers. The whole picture of James was crumbling before her eyes. The invincibility, the hard, polished perfection fading to reveal a small, dark-haired boy who had been loved less than a brutal bully. She understood the women, the harsh demands of desire. She even understood his need to protect her. James dared not love.

'Have I upset you?' Hester's gentle voice penetrated Gemma's own shocked thoughts and she looked up, tears shimmering at the back of her eyes.

'No. I understand now.'

'Because he never speaks of love?' Hester asked astutely. 'I've watched you both, my dear. I've seen his attitude.'

'He says he needs me.' With no one to talk to, no mother of her own, Gemma felt the need to almost beg for help, and Hester came to sit beside her, covering Gemma's hand with her own.

'Perhaps that's as close as James will ever get to confessing love,' she suggested softly. 'I've known him since he was nineteen and it was a long time before he told me anything. In all that time, I've never heard him confess to a need.'

'I—I'm not sure what sort of a need,' Gemma whispered. 'James wants to marry me but there are other women. Even now he's gone off with Miss Radcliffe to...'

'Indeed he has not!' Hester looked quite taken aback and then amused. 'That's what he told you? I thought I could hear him handing out some of those biting sentences. I *have* seen him in action at times over the years.' She got up and rang the bell. 'We'll have some tea, I think.' Her eyes sparkled at Gemma. 'James has gone to collect something for me. Miss Radcliffe has gone to visit friends, in the opposite direction. She did consider abandoning them when she knew you were out of action, but James in a bad mood is not exactly encouraging.'

It was astonishing how the news made Gemma's spirits rise, and quite ridiculous also. There was something between James and Sheena, she knew it, and nothing would cancel out Roma Prescott. All the same it was useless to pretend that life hadn't brightened.

When he came in later, he scowled at her. Apparently his irritation was too great to allow him to be pleasant enough to fool his aunt—not that Hester was easily fooled, as Gemma had found out.

'You realise, James, that we'll have the usual gathering tonight?' Hester said after watching them wryly.

'I expected it.'

'We normally have friends over on the evening of Christmas day,' Hester informed Gemma. 'We have a few drinks and a get-together. Then tomorrow we go to other houses. It's a little social round to make up for the lack of a tree and pretty baubles. Normally we give our presents out just before they arrive.'

Gemma carefully avoided looking at James. It took her mind back to other Christmases, the carefully chosen presents James had brought and her own equally careful refusal to buy one for him. This year she had given it a lot of thought. He had been kind to her, helped her, and she had enjoyed searching for something he might want.

It hadn't been easy either. There wasn't much he didn't already have, but her small time at his flat had given her an idea and she had the gift right now, carefully wrapped up and hidden in her luggage. Now that she understood about him it seemed terribly important to be able to give it.

Sheena was back before then. Gemma went to her room to get ready and selected a dark blue chiffon dress. It had a round neck and long sleeves, a full, flowing skirt over a satin sheath. Normally it would have made her feel quite glamorous, but not tonight. She was nervous, afraid to meet James and act out any loving relationship in front of other people.

When she went to the long drawing-room that faced the sea, Sheena was already there. So was James, and Gemma's heart sank. There was no denying Sheena Radcliffe's glamour. In a white, tight-fitting dress she looked anything but a nurse, and for a moment Gemma didn't know what to do as they both stared at her.

'Champagne, Gemma?' James asked, walking across to get her a drink. 'We have our little toast before the hordes arrive.'

'Not hordes, please, James,' Hester laughed, coming in then. 'I couldn't cope with hordes and the buffet wouldn't stretch to it. A *few* friends, Gemma,' she added. 'Don't let him intimidate you.'

'How could I?' James asked drily. 'Gemma is an accomplished hostess. She's used to running a huge house and dealing with anything from business lunches to week-long parties. She now runs my office very efficiently too.

Don't let her delicate looks fool you. Gemma can just about cope with anything, including me.'

The back-handed praise didn't seem to please Sheena much, her visions of a wishy-washy fiancée somewhat squashed. It amused Hester, though, especially as it was delivered with more accusation than praise.

'Present time,' she announced with all the glee of a child. 'I love this part best of all.'

Clearly she did and she was soon sitting on the settee, surrounded by gifts, the two servants coming in with wide grins to offer theirs. James looked surprised when Gemma walked to her room and came back with perfume for Sheena and a truly lovely piece of costume jewellery for Hester.

'I couldn't afford diamonds,' she smiled as Hester pinned the brooch to her dress.

'My dear, it's beautiful, though how you knew what to choose...?'

'I assumed that James would have an elegant aunt,' Gemma confessed, and it made James look at her very closely. No doubt he thought it was sarcasm. She gave him his gift before her nerve broke—a flat, carefully wrapped package she had lived in dread of damaging, or having to declare.

The look on his face was stunning and for a moment he didn't open it.

'For *me*, Gemma? You carried this all the way here for *me*?'

It almost made her cry and she trembled at the idea that she would have either overdone things or reminded him that she had never wanted to give him anything before.

'I had to carry it. I knew there wouldn't be time when we got here.' Hopefully her matter-of-fact voice would fool him and she had no idea whether it had or not when he unwrapped the gift. His attitude had succeeded in bringing all eyes to them and she felt pretty much like a child offering an aloof headmaster an apple.

It was a very good Monet print, beautifully framed, and he just stared at it until Gemma's face flushed anxiously.

'D-don't you like it?'

He looked at her through glittering, narrowed eyes, and his aunt jumped up to look for herself.

'It's beautiful, Gemma! This must be worth a great deal.'

'It—it took a bit of finding to get the r-right colours, but if James l-likes it...'

'Don't stammer, darling,' he said quietly, coming across to her. 'I like it.' His eyes searched her flushed face, looking for more than she was prepared to show. 'I suppose you've picked out the exact place for it at Brightways?'

'No. It's for your flat. Perhaps in the hall?'

'Or even over the bed,' he suggested softly. 'Thank you.' Right in front of his aunt's pleased face and Sheena's hard eyes, he slid one arm round Gemma and kissed her lips thoroughly. She could feel a tension in him and she longed to put her arms around him and beg forgiveness.

James gave her a bracelet to match the necklace he had already given her, and she was so stunned with her own success as Father Christmas that she never even noticed what the others got. Throughout the evening she felt his eyes on her wherever she moved. Soon after the gifts had been exchanged, a merry party of friends of all ages arrived and the engagement was thoroughly celebrated, although one or two of the younger men stated their disappointment openly.

'Come for a breath of air.' James issued the invitation as an order when Gemma found herself almost backed into a corner by one admiring male. The stiff smile he threw at the offender made resistance impossible and Gemma found herself out at the end of the cooler veranda in seconds.

'We can't just stay out here,' she got in quickly. He looked a little too intense and she was still reeling from so many things.

'I don't like people pawing you,' he muttered angrily. 'It robs me of Christmas spirit.'

'Surely I'm allowed the same privileges that you have in this modern world?' Gemma asked quietly. 'Most of the time you've been surrounded by ladies. Sheena actually surrounded you all by herself at one time.'

He suddenly laughed and swung her towards him, his dark eyes glittering down at her.

'I hope you realise just what that says to me. We're still watching each other intently, both jealous.'

'Of course I'm not,' Gemma lied gamely, looking straight at him. Her talk with his aunt had completely changed her attitude because now she understood, but she was not about to let James know. His hold on her was already too great.

'We'll not argue about it.' He pulled her into his arms, satisfaction on his face when she didn't attempt to break free. 'I'm going to ask you an indelicate question,' he confessed. 'I know it just isn't done but curiosity is killing me. How did you afford that Monet print?'

'It wasn't very expensive.'

'Gemma!' he warned softly. 'I'm not an uneducated lout. I recognise value when I see it. As I understood it, you were quite broke, considering taking a cheap flat and making ends meet. Now you've produced an expensive gift. How?'

'I—I sold a ring my father gave me,' she confessed, adding hastily, 'I needed something more suitable to wear for work.'

'When you became an important personal assistant?' he helped, making her feel like a stage-struck fool.

'Yes!' She looked up at him defiantly and his lips quirked with maddening amusement.

'So you bought yourself an office wardrobe?' he probed steadily.

'No.' She ducked her head. 'I—I saw the print and—and...'

'I really will have to cure you of that little stammer,' he said softly, tilting her face. 'I'll also have to do something about the lies you tell.' She struggled briefly but he merely tightened her to him, holding her gaze. 'You catch fire when I hold you. You give up things for yourself to buy me a present and you don't care about me, Gemma?'

It was not much use denying it and she was still smarting from the way she had acted before, the way she had hurt him without thinking. She turned her face against his chest, hiding from his eyes.

'I do care about you. I can't seem to help it. I won't marry you, though, James. All those women...'

'Have we reached a stage of discussion?' he asked softly.

'What is there to discuss? I even understand.'

'Do you, Gemma? I wonder how much you understand?' He tilted her face back to his, his mouth catching hers in a kiss that was altogether gentle and melted her soul. If they had been alone she would not have had any resistance in her, but the noise of the party was all around them and Hester popped out right at that moment.

'Oh! I'm so sorry, James. I had no intention of prying.'

It was so blatantly untrue, Hester's pleased looks making it quite plain that she wanted to see if things were all right, that any embarrassment fled from Gemma.

James was not very embarrassable in any case. He simply kept Gemma in his arms and turned to his aunt.

'We're going home, Hester,' he said quietly. 'We're going tomorrow.'

'All right, dear. I know you'll both be here again soon. Come inside and help out now, though—when Gemma has her breath back.'

She disappeared again and James tilted Gemma's face to the moonlight.

'Come back to London with me,' he murmured. 'We can't talk here. Hester is like Cupid. I want you to myself.'

'All right.' She knew exactly what she was agreeing to but it didn't matter.

She loved James.

They arrived back in London to find the biting weather still there. The cold had been easy to forget while they had been in Bermuda but it made itself felt at once and the sky was still that threatening leaden colour it had been when they had left.

James drove straight to his flat. It was still early enough in the day to make the trip to Brightways and he looked at Gemma's rather anxious face.

'A discussion, no more. I have no seduction scene in mind. I'll give you lunch and then drive you back to Brightways.'

She nodded her agreement, wondering if Jessie would be back, wondering if she had even been away at all. Everyone seemed quite happy to conspire as far as James was concerned.

The telephone was ringing insistently as they walked in and James picked it up with an air of extreme impatience. After listening, though, his expression changed.

'When?' He snapped out the word and Gemma knew it was some emergency. His face told her even before he replaced the receiver and looked across.

'I have to go, Gemma,' he said tautly. 'Get me on the next flight to Madrid.'

'What is it?' Even as she moved to the phone he was walking across to his room, taking off his coat and unbuttoning his shirt.

'The big complex we're building on the south coast of Spain. Suddenly we don't have planning permission any more, which is pretty damned annoying, as the thing is halfway finished. Bureaucracy gone mad. They've even given us a deadline before we take it down. Obviously there's some mix-up but I'll have to go and sort it out.'

He strode out of the room and Gemma lifted the phone, starting the procedure that would get him on his way. Nothing would hold James back. She knew that; and he wouldn't take her with him, she knew that, too.

There was a flight in an hour. She booked his seat and told him as he came back in, changed and ready, a small bag in his hand.

'Do you want to stay here until I get back?' he asked, but she shook her head. She wasn't ready for any commitment like that and, in any case, Jessie would soon be at Brightways.

'All right.' He didn't look too concerned. With this emergency, she had gone right out of his thoughts. 'Take the Mercedes. I'll collect it when I get back.'

It gave her the courage to take off the engagement ring and offer it to him.

'Where shall I put this?' Trying to be matter-of-fact when she felt so wretched was not easy but she managed it, and James looked at her steadily.

'How about back on your finger?'

'I can't wear it, James. It was only for your aunt and now she's not here.'

He turned away impatiently, more anxious to be off than anything else.

'Leave it on the desk, then.'

His attitude to so much value quite shocked Gemma and she stared at him in astonishment.

'Just on the desk? It's valuable!'

'Unless you are wearing it, it has no value at all.' His voice was as hard as his face and he simply took the ring from her hand and put it on the desk with the same impatience he had shown since his phone call. 'Let's go.'

No sooner were they in than they seemed to be going out and Gemma drove him to the airport.

'How long...?'

'God knows! I'll let you know.' He took a key from his key-ring and handed it to her. 'This is a spare key for the flat.'

'I don't need it. I won't be——'

'Take it!' He looked quite savage before he turned away. He just walked off, and after a few mournful minutes Gemma reversed the car to make her way out to the motorway and back to Brightways. There was nothing she could do to help James. It would have been better to be back at work.

He phoned that night, just after Jessie got back.

'How are things?' Gemma tried not to sound too much like an anxious wife but she knew just how much any problems like this affected him. He wasn't one to tolerate inefficiency.

'Not as bad as I feared. Only one man in the muddle. Everyone else is as annoyed as I am. Don't expect me back for a few days, though.'

'What about clothes? You only took a small bag.'

'Believe me, they sell shirts in Spain,' he said drily. 'Failing that, I'll find a laundry. Having got that over, is Jess there yet?'

'Yes. She got back an hour ago. It's snowing now.'

'Is it?' he said grimly. 'More trouble for the sites. Take care on the roads.'

He just rang off. No soft words, no sign that he missed her. He probably didn't, anyway. He had called her 'darling' to please his aunt, 'sweetheart' when he was being sarcastic, but there would never be words of love from James.

CHAPTER TEN

IT WAS a relief to get back to work the next day and take up where she had left off. With James away, a lot more work fell on her shoulders, but Gemma never felt unable to cope. What she could not cope with was the loneliness of not seeing him, and he did not phone at all. There were several departments that heard from him, but never Gemma.

On the first evening she left his car at the flat, having to fight her own urge to go in there and simply breathe in the atmosphere of James. She did not succumb, though. She caught a train home and thereafter had her own car.

For a couple of days the snow came intermittently until there was a thin covering on the ground and the hills were cold and white. The roads were clear and she had no difficulty in getting to work in spite of Jessie's repeated warnings of disaster.

At the end of the week, however, she drove home in a blizzard, relieved to see the drive at Brightways and the lights of the house. On the way she had passed two accidents and had seen several cars that had simply slid off the road. The roaring fire in the drawing-room was more than welcome and she was very thankful that it was Friday. By Monday the roads would be cleared.

Jessie greeted her with broad smiles, hot tea and not one word about the weather until she had imparted her glad tidings.

'He's on his way back. I've got a message. He rang the office but you'd left. He took the three o'clock flight

169

from Madrid.' She looked at the clock, her face wreathed in smiles. 'I bet he's landing right now.'

A few weeks earlier, Gemma would never have believed the surge of excitement that hit her. James was coming home. Without him she had felt lost and, whatever happened, she would never be able to deny it. For a few wild moments she wished she had stayed at his flat and used the excuse of the weather to explain her decision. She didn't realise that her feelings were showing on her face until Jessie gave a self-satisfied 'I knew all along' smirk and walked off to get the meal.

Gemma had left work early because of the weather, and it was only five-thirty now, but she was hungry, keyed up and restless.

'I'll have a sandwich to keep me going till dinner,' she remarked, walking into the kitchen.

'Well, that's one of your better ideas,' Jessie agreed. 'I wondered if Mr Sanderson would be coming for dinner. We could hold it for a while if you're having a snack.'

'I'm sure he'll be going straight to his flat,' Gemma said. 'In any case, I very much doubt if he could get through to here. The roads are terrible. Much as you dote on him, you won't be seeing him.'

'Neither will you,' Jessie pointed out tartly. 'If you were married I wouldn't have to spend my time worrying about you on those roads, because Mr Sanderson would bring you home.'

'Road safety is not a good enough reason for marriage, Jessie,' Gemma observed drily.

'Moonstruck is, and that's what you are,' Jessie snapped, but Gemma felt she had won a few small points. She took her sandwiches back to the drawing-room and the cosy fire, a smile on her face. Suddenly things were all settled in her mind because she knew she would marry James the very next time he asked her. Life without him was just too grey and unhappy. For the first time in her life she could see her whole future and at the very centre of it was the tall, dark, dynamic figure of James. She couldn't pretend any more.

It was comfortable sitting by the fire; Gemma ate her sandwiches and then switched on the television, not really listening, but relaxed and warm. Accepting how she felt about James had altered things here too. There was no longer the stark loneliness to the house that had always been her home. Somehow she didn't need it any more. She wanted to start all over again, with James, in a house where they could make their own memories.

The news attracted her attention briefly but in reality her mind was miles away, her thoughts on James, and only the scenes of an airport on the screen brought her mind to any stage of alertness.

'We are just getting reports of a major air disaster. The three o'clock flight from Madrid to London has come down in the Pyrénées in a snow-storm. As yet we know nothing of any survivors. Here is the number to ring...'

For seconds Gemma sat staring, icy-cold and white to the lips.

'James. James.' She sat whispering his name, stunned, disbelieving and lost. Only the sound of Jessie coming into the room brought her back to life and then she was racing to the phone, the number that had come up on the screen indelibly written in her mind.

'He's crashed. The three o'clock flight from Madrid crashed!' Frantically trying to dial, she whispered the words to a white-faced Jessie. Her fingers wouldn't seem to work and Jessie came and took the phone from her hand. 'Are you sure, Jessie? Are you sure James was on that flight?'

'Aye, love. I'm sure. I wrote it down. What's the number?' When Gemma told her, the older woman rang but almost at once put the phone back on its rest. 'There's no tone. The lines might be down. They come right over the hills to here.'

'Then I'm going to London. I'll go to Heathrow and find out.'

'You'll never get through,' Jessie said agitatedly. 'You said that yourself.'

'I'll get through. I've got to. I can't just sit here and wait.'

'I'll come with you,' Jessie averred determinedly, but Gemma stopped her at once.

'No. I can't have you on my conscience too. I deserve this! I deserve it! I never let him know I love him. He didn't know, Jessie.'

She burst into bitter tears and the motherly arms came round her as if she were still a little girl.

'Then you'll tell him when you see him. I'll get your coat.'

Gemma felt numb as Jessie fastened her into her coat, muttering for her to take care.

'He's dead, Jessie,' she murmured dully.

'I reckon not,' Jessie said briskly. 'Let's face the worst when we know it for sure. It's a pity you haven't still got that big car of Mr Sanderson's. Just you take care now.'

It was almost impossible to see the giant trees in the drive. The whole landscape was obliterated by white. Once outside the gates it was like moving into an alien world, but with the wind behind her at least the wipers were able to cope with the driving snow.

Since she had driven in it had not stopped at all and it looked as if it would never stop. The conditions were appalling and Gemma was forced to slow to a mere crawl in no time. The motorway would be bad enough because then she would be turned head-on into the wind, but if she had not lived here all her life she would have not had the slightest idea where she was.

Even in the streets of the village there were cars that had stuck and been abandoned to the driving snow, and when she came to the major road the police were there, working their way down a long line of vehicles and turning them back. She wound her window down, ignoring the cold, waiting with a steely determination to get through.

'Where are you going, miss?' The policeman who came to her window after a few minutes looked almost like a snowman.

'On to the motorway.' She felt that any further words would somehow jeopardise her chance to get past him, but her chances were remote, in any case.

'No possibility, miss. I'll get you turned.' He straightened up and began to signal but she leaned further out, her hair thick with snow now.

'I won't turn. I've got to get to London!'

'That's the general idea they all have, miss,' he said grimly. 'All they've been getting, though, is stuck in drifts. It's taking all the resources we have to keep the motorway open, let alone these side-roads. You can't get through. I can't even allow you to try because you'll only add to the chaos.' He stared down at her crossly. 'I've had this conversation fifty times already.'

'I think I'm different,' Gemma said quietly. 'My fiancé has been in a plane crash and I've got to get through. The phone lines are down and I don't know whether . . .'

He looked hard at her, seeing her distressed face.

'Wait a minute.' He walked further forward to where a police Range Rover stood with flashing lights, and Gemma sat with her head bowed, hopelessness washing over her. As long as she could be moving, doing something, there seemed to be hope. When she stopped, her hopes died.

He was back in a minute, signalling her to pull out and pass the other cars.

'Follow the Range Rover,' he ordered, leaning in at the window. 'He'll get through, so just follow his tyre-tracks. If you stop, he'll come back and rescue you.'

'Thank you.' She was tearfully grateful and the policeman's voice was suddenly gruff.

'Good luck, miss.'

He waved her on and she slid her car in behind the police vehicle and followed almost mesmerised until the movement and the lights anaesthetised her mind. There was just the red tail-lights, the blue flashing beacon, the white driving snow and nothing else at all. The world seemed to have come to an end but if James had died it didn't matter if the world stopped spinning.

It was almost nine o'clock before she pulled into the elegantly quiet street where James had his flat. The old Georgian crescent nestled in snow and it was hardly touched because as any car passed its tracks were swiftly filled in by the falling flakes. It looked like a scene from an old Christmas card but Gemma sat bleakly staring out of the car before she summoned up the courage to go into the flat and the atmosphere that would sing to her of James.

Her trip to the airport had been fruitless. The Pyrénées were snowbound, the crash miles from any-where, and rescue teams were only just beginning to work. With the best will in the world they could only tell her that James had been booked on the flight, and she was advised to wait at home and ring every hour.

There was nothing further she could do but wait and pray. She drew the curtains and put on the lights, finding the heating control and turning up the temperature. She tried the phone but Brightways was still cut off. Jessie would be worried but there was nothing that could be done about that. Gemma's mind seemed to have gone blank and from time to time she shivered uncontrollably even though the heating responded swiftly to the controls and the flat became beautifully warm.

Wandering around looking at things, touching things that James had touched, was too heartbreaking, and finally she settled in the lovely drawing-room that overlooked the street. It was then that she saw the ring glittering on the desk, exactly where James had dropped it.

He had said that it had no value unless she wore it and she pushed it on to her finger now, tears glistening on her lashes. She would never take it off again, because it was real; James had wanted it to be real.

With nothing to do, the time dragged heavily and still she seemed to be capable only of watching the clock, waiting for an hour to pass so that she could ring the airport. When it was time it seemed that she had reached some golden goal and she lifted the receiver with trembling fingers, willing herself to dial the number and find out.

The sounds of the front door opening and closing stunned her for a minute and then she heard his voice, calling her name with a sort of astonished hope.

'Gemma?'

She dropped the phone back down as the door into the drawing-room opened and James was there, a breath of cold air from the snowy street coming in with him; and she couldn't believe it. Her mind was too shaken to encompass the fact that he was there, real, alive! She simply couldn't speak and he looked at her with dark, stunning eyes, some glitter of longing at the back of his gaze. He seemed to be tense with anxiety.

'I saw the lights on and the car outside as the taxi dropped me,' he explained slowly as if he dreaded her answer. 'Your car's covered with snow but I knew it was yours. Gemma...?'

She was standing perfectly still, staring at him, her hands on her hot cheeks, willing herself not to faint, not to cry. He had never looked so handsome, so tall and dark, so beloved. And there was pain and uncertainty in his wonderful dark eyes.

Everything shattered—her tight, cool grip on her life, her hidden fears, her silence, and she flew across to him, flinging herself into the arms that closed round her instantly.

'I thought you were dead. I thought I'd lost you. James! James!'

He drew her trembling body closer, a sigh shuddering through him as he rested his head against her silken hair. She could feel his heart hammering as she sobbed out her words and then he lifted her face, wiping the tears.

'You heard about the flight that came down,' he surmised quietly. 'I didn't know myself until my flight landed. I had no idea you would know.'

'It was on the television news. Jessie said you were on that flight. I couldn't phone for news, the lines were down.'

'I missed the plane, Gemma. I missed it by miles but I managed to get the flight after that.' He suddenly looked puzzled. 'You were at Brightways? But the roads are closed. I wanted to go there myself and got warned off.'

'I got a police escort,' Gemma managed in a shaken voice. 'When—when I told them, they were very good to me but I still couldn't find out anything b-because...'

'Oh, hell! I would have spared you this if I could.' His eyes fell on the ring that glittered on her finger but he said nothing at all except, 'Come and sit down. I'll try to get a message to Jess. She'll be worrying about you.'

'And you! She thinks you're wonderful.' Gemma sank back into a deep chair, her hands trembling and her voice still shaken. James grinned across at her, a peculiar happiness on his face that kept her eyes fiercely on him.

'It's only what I expect,' he assured her drily. 'I've been working on Jess for at least two years. A spy in the opposite camp is only sensible, after all.'

He phoned Colonel Brant at the Hall in the next village and his line was still open. Gemma had been too distraught to think of that herself; the colonel had been a friend for years and he would always help.

'He'll send a lad over,' James informed her, imitating the colonel's fruity voice perfectly. Then he looked at her pale face. 'Can I get you anything to eat?'

'I couldn't eat a thing.' She shook her fair head and then offered, 'I'll get something for you.'

'I ate on the plane.' He was just staring at her, a half-smile on his face, but she could do nothing but stare back. She wanted to run to him again, to hold him.

'D-don't say that word ever again. I—I don't w-want to hear.' She stopped, her cheeks flushing. 'I—I'm stammering.'

'Well, I've not cured you yet and, anyway, I'm beginning to like it. Stammer all you want.' He came slowly across and knelt in front of her, his hands coming to her slender waist. 'So you love me?' he asked softly and she didn't even try to deny it.

'Yes. I love you, James. I've loved you for ages but I wouldn't tell you. I was jealous and scared but it doesn't matter now because I thought I'd lost you and all I could think was that I'd never told you I love you. I know you'll never tell me the same thing, but it doesn't matter because...'

His arms came tightly round her and he looked up at her with dark, glittering eyes.

'I love you,' he said clearly. 'I've loved you since I first saw you. I need you so badly that you're all I ever think of.'

With careful ease, he leaned forward and caressed her cheek, tilting her face then to allow his lips to move down the length of her neck. He was being gentle, his lips merely skimming her skin, but his eyes were burning into her and Gemma surrendered as she had wanted to do so often, leaning towards him with a smothered little sigh.

Instantly his arms tightened and he stood, lifting her with him so that they stood close to each other, pressed together.

'You're wearing my ring,' he murmured against her skin, his dark head bent as he moved his lips over her tilted face. 'You're going to marry me?'

'If you want me still.'

'If I want you? Oh, Gemma. I've looked at you, waited for you, longed for you until I nearly went mad.'

He was watching the movement of his own hands as they traced the base of her neck and moved lower to the curving rise of her breasts, and she was unable to move, her breathing fast and uneven.

'Belong to me—now,' he said urgently. 'Belong to me, because you're mine and I'll never let you go.'

'I won't want to go,' she whispered against his lips.

He pulled down the zip of her woollen dress, letting it slide to the floor, his eyes running over her as she trembled in front of him. Her body was almost fragile in the white silk of her slip, the lacy top barely covering her. Her nipples showed dark and secret through the fine lace and his jaw clenched as he stared down at her.

'In my mind I own you already, but each time I look at you it's the first time.'

His breath was a harsh rasp in his throat as he pulled her tightly against him, his hands moving restlessly over her as he buried his face against the silken shine of her hair. Her breathing seemed to stop as he spoke and she looked up as he let her lean away to look deeply into her eyes. She was trembling almost uncontrollably, trying to stop her frantic heart from bursting, her lips parted, her eyes enormous.

He was being so careful, not forcing things, but her body was filled with rushing excitement, an almost frenzied desire to be joined to him. He tightened her to him until they were almost breathing the same breath and her breasts seemed to swell as he looked down at them. It snapped his last restraint and he buried his mouth in hers, draining her of anything she would give, his tongue moving in the sweet warmth.

'This time it will be heaven,' he whispered thickly. 'You'll never be left hurting inside again, darling.' His voice was dark as black velvet, possessive, filled with desire, and he tilted her face, his dark eyes holding hers as his hands slid over her. 'My beautiful Gemma.'

Talking was past as far as he was concerned and his lips covered hers completely as his arms closed around her, his fingers trailing down the length of her spine until she arched against him. The dark magic engulfed her.

He was perfect, powerful, intoxicating, part of some secret dream she had known about since she had first met him. Even with her eyes closed she could see him because her mind had always seen him and seen herself right here. Her arms coiled around his neck in surrender, all thoughts banished but one—to be close to him, to obey his every wish—and he made a low sound of gladness deep in his throat as he swept her up into strong arms, gathering her against him, his lips never leaving hers.

She felt her clothes being gently removed and then the bed cool and soft beneath her after James carried her to his room. His face was dark above her as he stripped off his clothes, his lips like honey as he bent repeatedly to kiss her, and she could not get enough of him, her arms clinging to him until he came beside her.

'Say it, Gemma, say it again,' he demanded huskily and she just looked into his eyes, drowning in the darkness.

'I love you. If I ever lost you . . .'

'You never will.' His lips closed over hers with a kiss that was power and tenderness all at the same time.

'Gemma! Gemma! Gemma!' he groaned.

Her senses were heightened at the skilled coaxing of his hands and she moaned softly as she felt his touch on her. Her own hands found his skin, glorying in the silk rasp of it that made her tremble.

'Touch me, sweetheart,' he said thickly. 'Show me how much you want this.'

He was hypnotising her with his voice and his eyes, overwhelming her with his dark power, and her hands did as he ordered, moving over the strong muscles of his chest, over the smooth planes of his shoulders, her eyes following their trembling movements, her breathing fast and painful. He was ensnaring her soul but she gave it up willingly and his smiling lips recognised it, the harshness leaving his dark face.

'Gemma,' he whispered. 'It's real. We're together.'

His hands cupped her breasts, his mouth moving over the throbbing satin mounds, his pleasure murmured in his throat as she arched wildly against him. His lips moved over her ribcage to her stomach, searching her skin, caressing and arousing, finding all the places to give her pleasure, and she was restless in his arms, poised and waiting for the unknown happening, the crescendo of rapture that only he could bring.

'James!' Her voice was a distracted whisper, her hands urging him closer, her fingers in the crisp darkness of his hair, and he looked down at her, his eyes holding hers.

'I've waited a long time, Gemma. Now I want you begging.'

She didn't know how much she would beg as he explored her body with lips and hands, bringing her to wild awareness and then easing her back until her cheeks were flushed with desire and flame seemed to be running in her veins.

Her small, tormented cries brought the soothing ministrations of his lips, first to her tingling, hurting breasts and later to the satin-smooth skin of her inner thighs. When his kisses moved deeper, more intimately, to the very core of her womanhood, she thrashed about beneath him, restrained by his hand, heavy and warm on her, his body trapping her legs.

'James!' She gave a wild, keening cry, her head moving from side to side in a torment of desire that was an agony and an excitement. 'James! I'm begging you!'

'Yes, my love. Now you are, now you're ready.'

He moved back over her, his dark eyes blazing, holding her pleading gaze as he entered her deeply. She was so acutely attuned to him that she felt no pain. She felt only his triumph and her own. She belonged to him, and her silken body closed round him, drawing him further in, trapping him in love.

His dark eyes had flared as he'd felt the shattering of her virginity, and now he too surrendered, moving strongly in her body, giving and receiving until they shot off the world together, his lips fused with hers.

'Don't leave me, James,' she pleaded as they came back together to the softly lighted room. 'Don't ever leave me. I want to be with you always. I can't manage to live if...'

He caught her closer, his whole being still demanding but so wonderfully soothing.

'You will be, my darling. You will be with me always,' he murmured huskily. He moved against her and his kisses deepened and lengthened until Gemma gave a surprised cry as desire tore again through her body, ready for the renewed thrust of his invasion. Her only desire was to please him, to grant every wish, every demand. She could feel his enjoyment and her own delight rose with each second, her soft, gasping cries driving him on, her body like honey, enclosing him, warm and tight, her skin like velvet against his, her mind only just hearing her name on his lips as she travelled down the same spiralling, star-filled road with him until they were spent and warm in each other's arms, his lips covering hers with exquisite tenderness.

'It's only just begun, darling,' he whispered huskily. 'There's no more hurting for either of us. We're together.' She was too exhausted with passion to speak, lying spent and drained beneath him, and he spoke her name softly.

'Gemma.' It was only at his insistence that she opened her eyes. She was still locked close to him, his body refusing to move from her, and she felt a wave of terrifying shyness to add to her other feelings.

'Look at me,' he commanded quietly and she obeyed, her face still flushed and wild, her cheeks hot.

'James. I—I don't want to talk,' she began shakily and he smiled down at her with possessive amusement, his hands stroking her smooth, flushed cheeks.

'Did I demand conversation?' he asked softly, his dark eyes sensuous.

'I—I feel—it's just that I feel shy.'

'I know.' He kissed her eyes, his lips on the velvet-soft lids and the thick, dark lashes. 'This is where I wanted you to be the first time I saw you.'

'Coming down the stairs at Brightways,' she remembered with a sigh.

'No.' He shook his dark head. 'Months before then.' He rolled away from her, pulling her into his arms, his hand possessive on her stomach. 'I was just going out for a flight to New York and I saw you with your father. He had just landed and you were there to meet him.' He lifted her face to look at her. 'I never took my flight. I just followed you.'

'Followed me?'

He smiled and kissed the tip of her nose.

'I followed both of you. When your car pulled into the drive at Brightways I was right behind you. I went down to the village then and did a little detective work and I found that Barry Lyle of Lyle Engineering lived at the lovely old house and with him lived his daughter, Gemma.'

'So nothing was just an accident?'

'No,' he confessed. 'I couldn't afford to wait for chance. I'd fallen in love for the first time in my life and it was very painful. It was more painful still when you clearly hated me on sight.'

'I only thought I did,' Gemma said softly, her hand tracing his face.

'You fooled me nicely,' he assured her wryly, kissing her slender fingers. 'I just couldn't give up, though. It would have been like surrendering my soul. I got a partnership in Lyle Engineering, although I didn't need it at all—I already had more than enough to do with my own firm. That's when I found out about your father's lifestyle,' he added quietly, 'and there was nothing I could do to stop him. He was hell-bent on self-destruction and I knew what it would do to you when you found out. I had to stay as close as I could.'

'You said you would never love me,' Gemma reminded him.

'It was the only thing you seemed likely to believe. Any confession of adoration would have scared you to death. I had to be what I had always been: hard, cruel...'

'And invincible,' Gemma assisted.

'Oh, I'm all of that,' he grinned. 'Look where it got me. Subterfuge is my middle name.' He turned her to face him. 'When will you marry me?'

'Soon. Tonight if we could.'

She said nothing of her fears, and none of them were gone—it was just that her love had overwhelmed them—but James seemed to feel her small and secret withdrawal from him and he sat up.

'I can't take you out for a meal,' he pointed out. 'It's too cold. We can celebrate here, though. The freezer is well stocked and I have a daily who comes in and keeps the fridge up to date, among other things. I'll cook you a gourmet meal.'

Gemma had never seen him light-hearted before and suddenly her shyness vanished. She got up to stand in front of him, hindering him as he dressed.

'I'll cook,' she insisted. 'I'm a very good cook. I could take a job as a really exclusive housekeeper.'

'You've got a job,' he growled, pulling her against him, and she wound her slender arms round his neck. 'You'll soon have two. You'll have to choose which one you want most.'

He was roughly playful but she knew he had felt her slight unease, and everything was too new to talk about it to him. They made the meal together and for the first time they were at one with each other, stopping in the middle of cooking to kiss and caress. She had never felt like this before, never been so happy. She pushed the threatening clouds to the back of her horizon.

When Gemma awoke next morning, James was still sleeping, his hair tousled almost boyishly, his wonderful face relaxed. He looked sensuous, satisfied, and her cheeks flooded with soft colour as she remembered how much he had wanted her.

In the night he had lifted her into his arms again, his hands tracing her skin, his lips murmuring her name, and she had turned to him willingly, a slave to his every demand, his urgency thrilling, their lovemaking frantic until they had finally fallen into a soft sleep again, locked in each other's arms.

She could not believe how one long night could have changed her life. He had turned her into another being, and she had clung to him tightly, murmuring against his skin, and now as she looked down at him, raising herself on one elbow, she could only see the James she adored. She had known for a long time that he was a dark power and now she knew why. She had belonged to him since they had first met, as he had told her often in the night.

He opened his eyes to find her watching him, and the sensuous smile edged his lips as he drew her close.

'Now, who are you?' he murmured against her ear.

'You know who I am.' The dark, velvet voice made her shiver and she buried her face against him, almost afraid to speak.

'I've always known,' he pointed out softly. 'I'll be completely happy when I'm sure that you know. Tired?' he asked seductively, his tongue exploring her ear.

'A little,' she whispered, and he bent his head, finding her lips.

'It doesn't matter. You're staying here. Unfortunately I have to go and see what state things are in, but you are not moving from the flat. I might be very busy today. I haven't time to wander round finding you. Jess can cope. You're staying with me until we both go to Brightways together. It's not going to be today, even if the snow were to clear magically. I want you to myself.'

'Your cleaner,' she started anxiously, but he lifted her and pulled her down to him, trapping her in his arms.

'You're worried about convention? She doesn't come in today, as it happens. You can race round with a duster and then rest. I expect my lunch to be served promptly at one.'

'I'm not a slave!' She looked down at him with smiling defiance, her face flushing as he pulled her close to his sensuous lips.

'Are you sure? It's not the impression I got last night.'

'I—I've got to get up,' she said tremulously.

'Right now?' he asked, his teeth nipping her skin. 'I'm going to start the day as I've wanted to start it for over two years—with you in my arms.'

'James. I—I have to talk to you.'

When he saw her anxious looks the desire died out of his eyes and he rested her back against the pillows, coming to lean over her.

'I expected it. You want to make rules?'

'I love you too much to share you,' she whispered. 'I understand about the women, but James...'

'You've never shared me,' he said intently. 'Oh, yes, there have been women, but not after I saw you. From the moment I saw you my life changed. I couldn't offer you innocence but I could damned well change, and I did. In any case,' he added ruefully, 'I couldn't have you so I didn't want anyone else. There are no women, my sweet Gemma, and there never will be—only you.'

'But Roma.'

He laughed and looked down into her rather annoyed eyes.

'Yes, Roma,' he murmured. 'She is not, never has been and never will be my mistress. The speculation of the Press is quite without foundation. Roma is all push, and what she wanted was money—mine. She had big ideas and plenty of plans for the future—*her* future.'

'You *told* me she was your mistress,' Gemma said hotly, her eyes turning to a very dark purple, flashing with annoyance. He lifted her hand to his lips and kissed it lingeringly.

'Only shout at me quietly, darling,' he pleaded in amusement. 'I wanted you to be jealous and finally you were. I also wanted to hide behind her and, you've got to admit, she's a tough lady.'

'Well, there's Sheena Radcliffe,' Gemma pouted. 'You knew her before.'

'Before what?' he enquired, highly amused at her anger. 'I got her from an agency, at Hester's special request. Until then I'd never set eyes on her. She's Hester's nurse.'

'But she became a lot more to you, I think,' Gemma probed, only partly mollified.

'In my aunt's house? I'm shocked at your imagination, Miss Lyle!'

Gemma blushed and he laughed delightedly, pulling her into his arms.

'From the moment I saw you,' he whispered, 'there has been no one but you. I belong to you, Gemma, and to no other woman. I'll never look at one.'

She cuddled close, warm and at peace, and after a minute she stretched languorously and smiled mischievously into his eyes.

'You realise I might be pregnant?' she asked softly.

'It crossed my mind.' He looked at her vibrantly. 'I want you to myself for a long time yet but I was too desperate to think of it last night.' He smiled ruefully. 'On the other hand, I want to stamp my mark on you. I want everyone to know you're mine, and what better way?'

'Would you say that you're spoiled for choice?' Gemma asked smartly.

'I believe I am.' He kissed her soft and willing lips. 'At least Jess will be happy. Happier still when we're married and at Brightways.'

'Is that what you really want?' Gemma asked, her lovely eyes searching his face. 'Does Brightways mean so much to you?'

James looked at her for a long time and then leaned forward to kiss her tenderly.

'Tell me what's on your mind.'

'I used to think that the house was the very centre of my life,' Gemma told him softly. 'In many ways it was because it was all I really knew. It was what I came back to. Do you understand, James?'

'I understand, darling. And now?'

'Now there's you and another life. Maybe we should buy our own house, make our own dreams, our own memories.'

'If it's what you want.' He stroked her face, looking deeply into her eyes. 'To me, the house was you, the place where you lived, the only place I could see you. I wanted it so that I could enclose you in it, my dream.'

'I'm real, James. I'm not a dream and I love you.'

'Then I know just the place. As soon as possible we'll go to see it. It's big enough to hold a family but not big enough to be lonely, with plenty of room for Jess and any amount of children.'

Gemma stretched lazily and then slid out of bed, reaching for the robe she had worn the night before.

'I think I'll make some coffee. I wasn't too impressed by the coffee you made last night.'

'It's one of the few things I don't do brilliantly,' he explained, watching her with sensuous eyes. 'I'll stay here while you serve your lord and master.' He ducked, laughing, as Gemma threw a pillow at his head.

'I'll try to please,' she informed him tartly. 'Anyway, it's time for my assessment, isn't it?'

He caught her hand, pulling her to the bed and into his arms. 'You passed, with flying colours,' he whispered against her lips.

'There was an exam?' She looked up at him with dancing eyes.

'Hmm,' he murmured seductively. He was suddenly serious, holding her close. 'When you challenged me to let you have your chance I did some pretty quick thinking. I banked on your having the nerve to fight and, if you did, I knew you would come out of the small, sheltered world you inhabited. There would then be a chance that you might look at me.'

Gemma lay in his arms, her slender hand stroking back the dark hair.

'My deal with the devil,' she murmured. 'I'm so happy, James. I'll keep on trying hard at work, too, really I will. I'll never take advantage of our relationship.'

There was a lot of devilry in Gemma, as James was finding out, and his astounded expression was reward enough for her. She burst into peals of laughter and he frowned down at her, his own lips quirking.

'I'll have plenty of things to keep you occupied at home,' he said severely. 'I'd like my coffee now, and, as to the office, Miss Lyle—you're fired!'

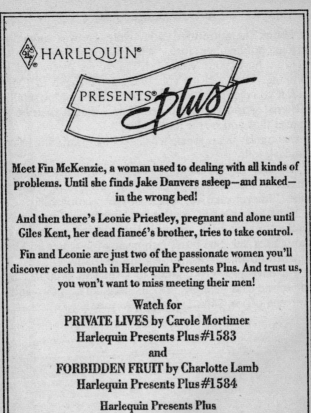